Something's Broken

Something's Broken

Nathan Jay

CONTENTS

– | VII |

The Birth of Alicia

I was only five years old when I shoplifted for the first time. I didn't realize I'd done it until I was riding home with my dad in his old LTD. There I was, sitting on the burning hot backseat, dangling my legs to the sounds of Curtis Mayfield and yanking at the candy wrapper with my teeth. Dad wasn't paying much attention to me. He was too busy riding through the streets, counting red lights and stop signs, trying to assign each to memory so he wouldn't have to ask for directions. We had moved from Washington, DC, to Asheville, North Carolina, because Daddy had accepted a job in a factory.

When we stopped at a stoplight, I tore into the candy wrapper anew, determined to get to the sweet chocolate inside. The crinkling of the wrapper got my dad's attention, and he turned around.

"What the…" he asked as he stared at me. "Where'd you get that?"

"The store," I responded.

My father's question didn't send up any alarms in my mind. The boxes of candy were in front of the cash register. Naturally, I grabbed one.

"You have to pay for that!" he yelled as he fought to keep from laughing. "Taking something without paying for it is stealing."

I stared at my dad with a blank look on my face. The concept of paying for things was as foreign to me as Algebra.

"I didn't steal it, Daddy. The candy was right there for me to take it. Boxes of it."

The statement pushed Daddy over the edge. Unable to stop himself, he burst into laughter. I started laughing, too. I mean, Daddy's laughter was as infectious as chickenpox. He reached back and yanked the candy bar out of my small hands. My laughter instantly became a frown of protest. Daddy tossed the partially eaten candy bar onto the front seat and made a U-turn.

"We have to go back and pay for that, Chuckles. We don't have any thieves in our house."

"But Daddy. I didn't steal anything."

"Hush, Chuckles. We're going back, and that's the end of it."

Minutes later, we were standing in front of the Store Manager.

"Sir, we're coming back because my little one took something that didn't belong to her," my dad explained.

The tall, middle-aged white man with rimmed spectacles looked down at us suspiciously. Although he wasn't tall, Daddy had this gigantic afro that made him look like a walking eraser. Long sideburns stretched down from his ears and disappeared into a thick black beard. He wore a shirt covered in different colored roses, and his pants were huge bell-bottoms that hugged his muscular thighs like spandex and then ballooned to hide his feet. Me? I was dressed in a simple striped short-sleeved shirt and faded jeans. Nothing spectacular. In my opinion, our presence was as regular as any other father and daughter. But the way the store manager stared at us made me uncomfortable – even back then. He looked at us like we were invaders, like Black Panthers coming to rob and kill everyone in the store.

"She stole something, huh?" the white man asked as he lowered his glasses to look down at me. "We prosecute all thieves in this store."

Daddy winked at the store owner and squeezed my small hand; I had gotten distracted by a large wire box filled with various colored rubber balls.

"That's what I told her, Sir. It's a lesson I wanted to get across to her. A person always pays their debts."

I looked up at the tall white man and then lowered my head in shame. I didn't want to be a thief. I did believe the candy bars were there for the taking. I didn't know I had to pay for them.

What the man said next was both confusing and terrifying.

"We've had a lot of problems with the Blacks coming in here and stealing. I reckon we ought to make a lesson out of one or two of you to show the rest not to mess around in here."

Daddy looked down at me and then shot the man a look as if to say - I'm trying to teach my little girl a lesson, and you go and ruin it with your foul mouth? But the man wasn't finished. He turned to the raised desk at the grocery store entrance.

"Natalie. Call the police."

Daddy instantly objected.

"Now hold on, Sir. I just wanted to teach my daughter a lesson. You're taking things too far."

"You're goddamned right I'm taking things too far. The next time, you'll keep that little monkey in line."

The look of hurt that came across Daddy's face was something I've never been able to forget. He wanted to destroy the racist store manager – I could see it in his eyes, and I could feel it in the tightened grip on my little hand. But my dad wasn't a fool. He knew an escalation would surely mean his Chuckles would be in danger.

Daddy dug into his back pocket and pulled out $2.00. He placed the two wrinkled bills on the counter of the nearest register.

"Here's your money for the candy bar. We'll be on our way now. Thank you kindly."

The manager instantly rejected the offer.

"What do you think this is? You can't go anywhere, boy," he snapped. "Natalie. Hold that boy at the entrance until the cops get here."

I couldn't see who Natalie was until she stepped from behind the tall desk. Natalie was a 250-pound store security guard with long blonde hair. Her round, chubby, freckled face and rosy cheeks were what I remembered the most about her. Her pants were too small for her thunderous thighs; they were so tight and looked like they would split if she bent over. She wore no police badges or plastic indicators showing that she was store security, only a ketchup stain indicating what she had been eating at lunch.

She walked up and stood in front of my dad. He looked like a child standing in front of the husky woman. Her presence was the reason the store hired her.

"Ma'am, if you please. I don't want any trouble. I want to go to my car and take my little girl home."

The store manager was having none of it.

"Hell no! Natalie, you hold that boy right there!"

I was crying at this point. The store manager frightened me. He wanted to take us to jail, and it was all my fault.

Suddenly, something happened that was so surprising that it jolted me.

Natalie winked at me!

"Sir, take your daughter and go home. There's no foul here," she said.

The store manager was so shocked at the words that he stood with his mouth open. My dad paused a moment to stare at Natalie. Eventually, he pulled me towards the exit.

"I thank you kindly, ma'am."

"No thanks needed. I'm sorry about this horrible experience. Please do shop with us again. Have a good day, Sir."

And then Natalie did it again – but she winked at my dad this time! This time, it was Daddy's turn to stare in amazement at the girl. After looking back and forth at the manager and Natalie, Daddy started moving towards the door. When Daddy and I took two steps, the manager was on Natalie like a hornet.

"Well, I'll be...you get that black..."

"Shut your mouth, Mr. Pritchard!" the woman bellowed. "Being a supervisor is not an excuse to treat customers like this!"

"How dare you! You're…"

"Fired? You don't have the power to fire me. My family owns this store. Just wait until I tell them how you treat customers."

Daddy tugged on my arm, and we moved through the store's automatic doors. Daddy kept looking back and laughing as we walked through the parking lot. He was like a giddy child. He kept repeating the same words over and over.

"Hot damn! Hot damn! Damn it! Damn it! Hot damn!" he exclaimed as he opened the door of the car for me to get in.

"Daddy. Why did the…"

"No time to talk now, Chuckles. Let's get out of here."

As we drove through the parking lot, I continued to look back at the grocery store. Daddy did too. I could see his gigantic afro smashed against the car's roof as he looked in the rearview mirror.

"Let that be a lesson to you, Chuckles. Stealing causes a lot of problems."

"But Daddy…"

"Hush now. We'll talk about it when we…"

Daddy was unable to finish his sentence. As we turned to exit the parking lot, two cop cars turned and headed toward the grocery store.

"Shit."

"What is it, Daddy?"

Daddy's voice changed. He began to stumble over his words.

"I'll bet you're mad at your old Dad, huh?"

"What?"

He kept looking in his rearview mirror.

"We just have to make it up to Tucker Lane," he whispered. I looked out the rear window of the car. I didn't see anyone behind us.

"Daddy, you're not making any sense."

He slapped at his chest until he found his pack of cigarettes. Afterward, he pushed in the lighter on the dashboard and waited for it to heat up.

"You okay, Chuckles?"

But I was scared, and I could tell something wasn't right. Daddy pulled out the lighter and lit his cigarette. After taking a deep puff, he looked in the rearview mirror again before blowing out a big cloud of smoke.

"That candy bar sure was good, huh?"

"Yeah. Where is it?"

"Let's get home, and I'll get it for you."

As we turned onto another street heading back home, we passed a patrol car at a stop sign. Daddy didn't even look in the direction of the police officers. He stopped and waited for a full five seconds before continuing his journey. The police pulled out behind us.

"Daddy," I said nervously.

"Don't worry, Chuckles. I see them. You sit tight and make sure you have that seatbelt on."

Soon, the blue lights of the police car flickered on. Daddy pulled over to the side of the street and turned off his engine.

"Just be calm, Chuckles. Let me do all the talking, okay?"

"Okay, Daddy."

Daddy put his cigarette in the ashtray and watched the two officers exit their vehicle.

"Everything's going to be okay, Chuckles. Don't worry," Daddy reassured me.

When the two police officers arrived, I knew there would be trouble.

"Sir, do you know why I'm stopping you today?"

"No, Sir. I was going the speed limit."

"One of your taillights is out."

"What?"

At that moment, I heard the smash against the back of our car.

"Daddy!" I yelled.

"Sir! Sir! I have my little girl with me. Please."

"Shut your goddamned mouth, boy. Get out of the car."

"But I haven't done anything."

"I'm not going to tell you again. Get out of the fucking car."

"But...what about my daughter? I can't just..."

I'll never forget the sound I heard. It was so sickening that I almost vomited in the back seat. The police officer hit my dad in the temple with his nightstick with such force that my dad's body slumped into the passenger's seat.

"Daddy! Daddy!" I screamed.

But he couldn't hear me. I watched in horror as the police officer opened the door, grabbed him by his belt, and pulled him out of the car. Daddy fell in a heap of pain onto the hot street.

My panic was automatic after seeing that. I couldn't stop yelling for my Daddy. With every breath I took, the temperature in the car rose higher and higher. I remember my shirt sticking to my back as I struggled to get a glimpse of Daddy lying on the ground. I was sure he was dead.

Suddenly, like a terrifying ghost, the police officer who assaulted my dad stuck his head into the car. Seeing him was like seeing the devil. All the oxygen disappeared out of the vehicle. I remember jumping at the sight of the man, slamming my shoulder hard against the car door, and remaining plastered against it in fear. His red hair looked like greasy strands of puke stuck to the side of his head. Drops of sweat crept from underneath his hat and down the side of his freckled cheek.

"Shut your fucking mouth, you little bitch! Shut up right now, or I'll give you a taste!" he hissed.

I could tell the cop enjoyed the power he had at that moment. A Black man was bleeding out at his feet; the victim's daughter was imprisoned in a hot backseat - shivering within the violent atmosphere, and the child knew he had the power to send her tiny soul screaming into the afterlife. I could see it in his eyes. That moment excited him. It pushed him. I could see his evil brown eyes searching the hot car for a reason — any reason, to unleash hell on the nigger-child in the back seat. He reveled in the atmosphere he created. All of it. The blood. The graphic violence against the child. The heat of the day. I saw it all in his eyes at that moment.

But at that point, I couldn't stop crying if I wanted to. All I could think of was Daddy lying on the ground. Suddenly, there was a voice yelling from behind the car.

"Jesus, Shipman! She's a baby! What the hell are you doing? We were supposed to scare him, not fucking kill him!"

"Shut up, Dex. When I want your opinion, I'll give it to you!"

The other officer walked to the driver's side of the car and looked at my dad lying on the ground. Blood was pouring from his head, and he was twitching.

"Let's get out of here. This guy is fucked up. You caved in his skull. Let's go before someone calls it in."

Officer Shipman took one final look at my father and started backing away.

"Stupid fucking niggers just don't know how to listen. Now your skull's crushed. Stupid son of a bitch!"

The officers ran back to their squad car. After making sure no one had seen what they had done, they gunned their engine and left my dad lying on the hot pavement with blood pouring from his head. And me – stuck in the back of the burning car, crying my eyes out in terror.

2

The Birth of Julian

On my 6th birthday, I received a BMX bike from Ms. Hicks, the woman who lived next door to ours. Mom told me that it was a gift that Ms. Hicks paid for through layaway at Walmart. According to my mom, quite a feat and worthy of a show of gratitude (mom made sure that Ms. Hicks saw me riding that bike every day). Although I was grateful to be one of the few kids in the neighborhood to receive such an awesome toy, I was still old enough to understand what it was; a pay-off from Ms. Hicks to me, a purchase of silence for what went on in her bedroom when mom was at work.

I had to call her Ms. Hicks, but my mom and every other adult called her by her nickname: Dori. The childless 40-year-old divorced woman used to watch me while my mother balanced two jobs. She possessed all the same things that most of my mom's friends did back then; a mild-mannered personality, a position that barely paid the rent, a fondness for drinking beer on Fridays, and a willingness to talk shit with my mom.

In the beginning, she seemed like a decent person to me. I liked her braids; there were hundreds of them all over her head, all with tiny white beads attached. Her voice was soft and often smelled like she'd put on too much cheap perfume. When she laughed, she covered her mouth to hide the large gap in her teeth, a present from her abusive ex-husband when she tried to stop him from taking her savings to blow on drinking and gambling (I'd overheard her telling my mom about it). On most days, she wore the same clothing. Her wardrobe consisted of low-budget items thrown together. A scarf from Woolworth's, different skirts my mom gave her whenever she felt guilty about the low salary she was paying her for babysitting me, several worn jeans, two or three pairs of shoes that were so old that they all had bumps from the corns on her feet.

While my mother worked, she ensured I did my homework and ate a decent dinner. After I finished, she'd let me watch television on this big black and white television in her bedroom. Although it was propped up with two phonebooks and had a coat hanger for an antenna, I felt special when she let me watch it; my mom didn't own a television, and I was usually bored out of my mind by staying home. It never occurred to me that she was softening my apprehension about entering her bedroom.

It started with a simple question:

"Julian, what's your girlfriend's name?"

You never understand how frightening a question like that is for a child until you've been in that situation. When she asked me, my emotions were all over the place. It's the equivalent of wanting to feel experienced yet broadcasting your innocence to the world all at once. You want to seem older than you are, yet you're almost willing to do anything to alleviate the intense interrogation of the person applying pressure.

"I don't have a girlfriend," I said truthfully. I didn't. So, what if she didn't believe me? I focused on watching the old television; cartoons were a premium in my world, and if I didn't take advantage of watching them, who knew when I might be able to see them again?

"I find that hard to believe. A handsome boy like you? Why is that?" she asked softly.

Pressure applied.

The room became smaller, and a feeling of unease crept over me. I stared harder at the television and shrugged my shoulders. Something wasn't right.

"Do you have a special friend?" she continued.

I focused even harder on the television. I began to object to Ms. Hick's questioning internally. Why couldn't she leave me alone? Who cared about a special friend? Were all adults this annoying?

"Julian, answer me. Do you want me to tell your mom you were misbehaving?" she asked.

More pressure.

Most people think that being an only child breeds spoiled children who get away with murder. Not in our house. Mom was a strict disciplinarian and didn't tolerate children mouthing off to responsible adults. She was a bit old school and clarified that if she received a phone call about me disobeying an adult, there would be hell to pay. Fearing mom's wrath, I gave in.

"No. I don't have a special friend," I murmured.

Satisfied with my response, Ms. Hicks stood up.

"You want a snack?"

I shook my head yes, and she left the room. Only the sound of cartoons played on the TV for a few minutes. I expected her to return immediately, but she didn't.

I got comfortable.

I forgot the intense questioning. It wasn't long before I laughed out loud at the cartoons on the old tv. I never heard the door open.

A woosh of violet flowered fabric was in front of me, and then the television turned off. I looked up to see Ms. Hicks. She held a saucer with cookies in her hand, and she had a glass of milk in her other hand.

"Here's your snack. Go sit on the bed," Ms. Hicks instructed.

It was at that moment that I noticed her nude breasts through her see-thru robe. I froze. I was both embarrassed and ashamed of what I saw. I didn't know why, but it felt like I'd barged into her bedroom while she dressed. The moment felt almost criminal on my part; I began to fear what my mother would do if she found out. Now that I think about it, that feeling was like standing on the ledge of a skyscraper, knowing you shouldn't be there and feeling the tug of gravity daring you to step off. I've never had a feeling like that since. That moment was so devastatingly arresting to my childhood.

I tried to do as she instructed, but I couldn't move. My eyes instantly fell on the old beat-up record player she had beside the tv. I remember the record on the spinner – The Sylvers, Only One Can Win. I stared at that record, hoping it would start playing. It didn't.

After a few seconds, Ms. Hicks became impatient.

"Go ahead, Julian. Get on the bed."

I'm unsure if it was the authority she added to her voice or if I just wanted to move away from her. Either way, my legs began moving. I didn't sit on the bed. Instead, I stood with my little rear pressed against its edge. Although nothing had happened, I prepared myself to run. I didn't look at Ms. Hicks, but I could sense her; she seemed to float about the room like a ghost wrapped in silk. She caressed the top of my head with her rough, calloused hands before sitting down on the bed beside me.

"Do you want to be my special friend?"

I bit into my cookie and chewed slowly. Ms. Hicks began to pepper me with questions; every negative response was tied to some physical interaction as if she was the positive side of the battery to generate the reaction she wanted. Every answer I gave seemed to open another of her trap doors, and I'd tumble in. After a while, I did whatever she asked. I accepted her explanation for our activities as gospel. She was an adult, and I was a kid. I felt crushed beneath the weight of her needs. She had her way with every part of me.

In time, my sexual interactions with Ms. Hicks became so routine that I almost knew what she wanted of me on command. Sometimes, she'd instruct me to go to her bedroom, and I would automatically walk into the darkness, stepping out of my clothing. The whole thing became robotic in my mind. Now that I think back on it, I was like a dildo. But instead of hiding me in her underwear drawer, I became a more interactive version of the sex toy; I did homework, ate cookies, and watched cartoons. There was no pleasure for me - curiosity, maybe. My body's reaction to certain activities she performed made me feel physically broken or, at a minimum, injured. There was no thorough explanation of the male body's response to sexual touch. There was only Ms. Hicks looming over me like a dark rain cloud, getting what she wanted from the abusive game before the clock expired and Mom came home.

Mom found out about Ms. Hicks and me how most mothers discover secrets in their home – through instinct. One day, I walked into her room while she dressed for church.

"Hey, boy! I'm getting dressed," mom snapped. But she didn't make any attempt to hide her body. In her mind, she was my mom, and I'd seen her mom-body hundreds of times. Except for this time, my response was a little different.

"You're not the first woman I've seen naked," I replied. Mom froze.

"What?"

I tried to cover my obvious blunder, but I did a horrible job of it.

"I mean... I've watched TV."

Mom didn't buy it. She looked at me suspiciously as she got dressed.

"You've seen a naked woman?"

"I mean..."

"Don't lie to me, Julian. Have you seen a woman naked?"

"I mean...yeah...I guess."

"Who was it?"

"Mom. It's okay."

"Was it Ms. Hicks? Is that the person you saw naked?"

"Mom...stop."

Mom let the subject slide but didn't stop applying pressure. Like a master surgeon, she continued picking at me throughout the week. While eating dinner, she'd say things like,

"That Jefferson boy that you play with got into a bit of trouble last week when he was skipping school. It turns out he had been skipping school for weeks. If only he and his mother had the kind of relationship you and I have. I know my son would never hide anything from me. Right?"

On top of picking at my conscience, mom used her culinary skills to chip away at the secret. One day, she made her world-famous I love you Burgers – a burger she created to help me get past the pain I had when Dad abandoned us. With each bite of her world-famous burgers, each person confessed a secret. If that person didn't reveal that secret, they could reply "later" to pass. By the time I finished my burger, I had so many passes I could've ridden for free on the bus for a year. To me, the "passes" were an escape. But to mom, each "pass" told her I was hiding something.

On the fourth day of her emotional interrogation, I revealed everything. Part of it was through a mother's quizzing of her son, but most of it was through a surprise visit mom made to Ms. Hick's house.

As Ms. Hicks ran me through her usual routine of "getting hers," there came a loud knock at the apartment door.

"Dori! Dori! Open up!" a voice yelled. Ms. Hicks looked terrified. It was my mom!

"Quick! Put on your clothes!" she instructed me. I fumbled in the dark to put on my underwear and jeans. At that moment, I was afraid, too. I knew what was happening was wrong, but I was terrified of damaging the trust mom had in me. She would see that I was hiding something from her.

"Dori!" Mom yelled from outside the apartment.

"I'm coming! Hold on!" replied Ms. Hicks.

She slid into her jeans and put on a t-shirt that was much too small for her.

"Go to the dining room table and open your schoolbook."

Obediently, I went downstairs and sat at the table. Seconds later, Ms. Hicks came down and opened the door.

"Shit, Christina!" she exclaimed as she yanked on the tight shirt. "What's going on? Is everything alright?"

Mom looked at Ms. Hicks suspiciously.

"Where's Julian?"

"I'm over here, mom."

I stood and walked to the door so my mom could see me.

And then it happened.

Mom's eyes moved away from Ms. Hick's eyes to her breasts; her long nipples looked like sharp pencils poking through the fabric of her shirt. She was still horny.

"What is it, Christina? What's going on?" asked Ms. Hicks.

But mom said nothing. She continued her inspection in silence. Her eyes moved from Ms. Hicks's breasts down the front of her jeans, jeans that, until that point, I hadn't noticed were wet in the crotch. After seeing Ms. Hicks's stained jeans, Mom grabbed my arm.

"Come on, Julian. Let's go."

"What's going on, Christina? What's wrong? At least let Julian get his books."

Reluctantly, Mom complied.

"Go get your books. Hurry up."

Ms. Hicks continued trying to get an explanation.

"Has there been an emergency or something?"

Mom ignored Ms. Hicks and watched me collect my things from the dining room table. She pulled me out of Ms. Hicks's apartment and walked into ours.

"Get in that bathroom and strip."

"What for mom?"

"Julian, do as I say! I won't tell you again!"

As I pulled off my shirt, mom started crying. Soon, I joined her.

"What's wrong, mom?"

"Take off your underwear."

"But mom, I..."

She didn't wait for me to do it. She yanked my underwear down around my ankles. Suddenly, Mom grabbed me by my arm and pulled me close. With her other free hand, she rubbed roughly across my genitals.

"Mom! What are you doing? Please! Stop!"

"Shut up!"

She pushed me towards the sink and lifted her hand to her nose. Suddenly, something exploded inside her, and she fell against the wall in tears. She began hyperventilating as she talked to me.

"Julian...you...{gasp}...get into the shower."

"Mom, what's wrong?"

"Do...as...I...say...{gasp}."

I climbed into the shower and turned on the water. The situation was so numbing that I didn't even know if I turned on the hot or cold water. Mom pulled the lid of the toilet down and sat on it. In time, she calmed enough to speak.

"Make sure you wash your ding-a-ling and butt."

I obediently scrubbed my body while mom sat there – waiting. I thought I was a goner for sure. Each spanking from mom was legendary, and I all but knew I would get one then. I'd kept a secret from her, and now she knew.

"Are you finished, Julian?"

"Yeah."

Reluctantly, I turned off the shower and climbed out. Mom was waiting with a towel in hand. After she dried me off, she ran her hand across my genitals again and sniffed.

"Get back in the shower. I'll wash you this time."

"But mom, I washed correctly."

"Julian, get in the fucking shower! Now!"

This time, when I got in, mom was rough. She lathered me up and scrubbed rigorously from head to toe. Mom cleaned areas of my body that I never knew a person could clean – all the while crying and cursing Ms. Hicks under her breath. I cried too. I had never seen my mother in such a state of utter pain.

After I dried off and dressed, Mom and I sat at the dining room table. Still expecting punishment, I stared at mom, waiting for her wrath. That's the thing about child abuse that many people don't understand; on top of being mistreated by adults, children punish themselves by thinking they did something wrong.

After sitting quietly for a few minutes, mom spoke.

"Julian. Now isn't the time for games. You need to tell me everything Dori did to you."

"Mom, I..."

"Baby, I'm on your side. You didn't do anything wrong. I'm not mad at you. I'm not. If Ms. Hicks did something to you, touched you..."

"I don't think..."

My voice trailed away. Although I was relieved Mom wasn't mad at me, I wanted to disappear from that table. How do you tell your mom about all the secrets you never discussed with anyone?

Mom reached out and grabbed my hand. I can still feel how her hand felt – trembling and clammy as if she'd just washed dishes.

"I love you, Julian. You are my child. There is no one on this earth that I love more than you. Talk to me, baby. What did she do?"

I searched her face, looking for a way out. I found a deep love that pulled me in like a warm blanket in a cold room. I stood up from the table and went to my mom's side.

"Can we sit in the living room with the lights turned off?"

"Sure, Baby."

Although it wasn't completely dark outside, I still tried to give myself cover in the few shadows in the living room. Mom stood up, and we walked to the sofa. We sat down, and I rested my head on her shoulder.

After a few minutes, I told her everything.

When all the secrets were out, and Mom was satisfied that she had the truth from me, she kissed me on my forehead.

"I'm so proud of you."

"Why?"

"Because it takes a big person to speak up when someone has hurt them. You showed a lot of courage."

I cracked a smile and hid my face in my mother's arms.

"I need you to do me a favor."

"What is it, mom?"

"Go to your room and finish your homework."

I could sense something wasn't right, but my little head was bad at detecting at that age.

"Are you going to cook?"

"Eventually. I need to go next door and tell Ms. Hicks she won't be watching you anymore."

I stood up, and Mom kissed me again.

"Do your homework, okay? We don't need any bad grades, right?"

"Right."

I walked to my room. I never saw the knife mom got from the kitchen.

When our front door opened, I was there, propelled by the fear of what my mom would say. She knocked lightly on Ms. Hicks's door. There was no answer.

"Dori, I know you're home. Let's talk about this before it gets any bigger. Neither of us needs drama."

No one answered the door.

"Fine, Dori. If you want me to go to the authorities..."

The door unlocked, and Ms. Hicks stuck her head out.

"No. There's no need for that," Ms. Hicks said. Her skin was pale, and streaks of mascara ran down her face. I guess she'd been crying.

"We need to talk. You want to do it out here or inside?" asked Mom. I could hear her voice trembling with anger. Ms. Hicks opened the door.

"Come on in."

As soon as she opened the door, my mother pounced. She grabbed Ms. Hicks by her hair and threw her into the wall.

"You fucking bitch!" she yelled. "Pedophile! I'll kill you!"

I ran to Ms. Hicks's apartment door.

"Mom!" I yelled. "Please stop!"

Mom's eyes looked wild, like she was possessed. She slammed her fists into the woman's face over and over.

"Touch my son? I'll kill you!"

Ms. Hicks held out her hands, but there was no stopping the assault.

"I'm sorry. Please. Please..."

But mom didn't stop. She grabbed the flowered lamp off the table and crashed it into the woman's scalp. Ms. Hicks's legs went limp, and she crumbled to the floor in agony. A strange sound escaped her throat. At the time, I didn't understand it. It wasn't a sound of pain or even a cry. It seemed more like acknowledging the events as if she knew her moment of judgment would arrive with my mom standing over her. It was almost like she was - relieved.

Suddenly, Mom stopped hitting the woman. She walked over to the door, looked around to ensure no spectators, and pulled me into the apartment. Ms. Hicks sat up on the floor and spat blood into her hand.

"I could have you put in prison."

"So...do it. Or kill me. I don't care anymore."

Mom walked over to Ms. Hicks, grabbed a handful of her hair, and yanked on it until her head slammed against the wall.

"Look at him!"

"Ow! I...can't...please..."

"I said, look at him, you pedophile bitch!"

When Ms. Hicks turned to look at me, I gasped in disbelief. One of her eyes was swollen shut.

"When you see Julian, you'd better fucking run! I mean, run to the other side of the road. You got that?"

"I got it."

"Do you? Because if you say hello or even look in his direction and I find out, I'll fucking kill you!"

Slowly, she let go of her hair and backed away.

"Let's go, son."

I took Mom by the hand and moved towards the door. Just as I opened it, she jerked her hand away from me.

"Fuck this!" she whispered. Mom reached into the back of her jeans and pulled out the butcher knife. Ms. Hicks's eyes widened.

"Wait! Wait! Wait!" she screamed.

Mom plunged the knife into the woman's leg with such force that items on the counter rattled. Blood was everywhere. Ms. Hicks grabbed her leg and screamed.

"AAAAAAHHHHH!"

Mom took a step back to observe what she'd done, a twisted smile of satisfaction.

"Go ahead. Call the cops," Mom said. "Tell them what I did, and I'll tell them what you did."

But Ms. Hicks wasn't concerned with what Mom was saying. Her face had turned as white as a sheet, and she started shaking uncontrollably. A big red puddle of blood spread out like a pool beneath her body. I was terrified. I was a kid, and even I knew she would die if we didn't do something.

"Mom!" I yelled. I grabbed the towel on the counter and tried rushing to help Ms. Hicks, but Mom pulled me back.

"Go home, Julian! I'll take care of this!"

"But mom! She's going to die!"

"Go home, Julian! Let me take care of this! Do as I say!"

I could see Ms. Hicks starting to sweat. Her head began to nod, and her eyes looked sleepy. I knew she was going to pass out. Mom snatched the towel from me.

"Go home, Julian!"

As I walked out of the apartment, Ms. Hicks let out a feeble scream. I turned around to see that my mom had pulled the knife out of her leg. Before closing the door, I saw mom attempting to stop Ms. Hicks's bleeding with the towel.

"You fucking bitch. I should let you die," she whispered as she took off her shirt, ripped it, and tied it around Ms. Hicks's leg. Satisfied with Mom's attempt to save the woman's life, I walked inside our apartment and sat at the dining room table.

I waited for Mom to burst through the door covered in blood.

I waited... And waited... And waited....

But she didn't come.

After a while, the whole world seemed to be outside our apartment door. The thunderous footsteps of dozens of men pounded the floor on their way to Ms. Hicks's apartment. There was yelling but no crying – which I found oddly inconsistent. I could hear the squeaking radios of the police officers. They talked in code while combing over the scene. Suddenly, I heard a voice much louder than the others.

"Ma'am, what's your name? Can you tell us what happened here?" the male voice asked. But there was no response.

"She's not speaking?" asked a female voice.

"No, nothing yet," responded the male voice. I didn't hear my mother's name mentioned, but I knew they were talking about her. I listened closely to see if I could hear Mom speaking. Instead, I heard the men using confusing words like "suspect," "custody," and "deceased."

I sat at that dining room table for hours; it was just me: obedient, lonely, afraid, waiting for Mom to come home. But she never came. It was early morning when my uncle came to check on me. By then, I was curled up asleep on the couch.

3

Alicia's High School Days

Alicia winced as her tiny body crashed into students passing in the opposite direction. Frustrated, she pushed her glasses up on her nose and held her books close to her chest. Football players, cheerleaders, and seemingly every annoying student at Fletcher High School bounced her around the hallway like a pinball. Alicia did her best to stay focused on her destination – locker 127-B. She had enough time to grab her books and sprint to the class. Mrs. Penney had already given her a final warning about her excessive tardiness. One more infraction and she'd be locked up in the worst of purgatories - summer school.

As soon as Alicia arrived at her locker, she started spinning the combination. Her first attempt failed to open the lock, then her second, and then her third. Finally, she let go of the dial and took a deep breath.

"Come on, girl. Get it together," she whispered. Once again, she spun the combinations on the dial until she finally heard a click.

"Great," Alicia said as she pulled it open. "It only took me a million tries."

After stuffing her Algebra and Science books into her locker, she grabbed her English books and slammed the locker shut. Just as she turned around, someone bumped into her, causing her to spill all her books onto the floor. Frustrated, Alicia began picking up the books from the ground.

"Look at Ms. Thing heading to class," said a deep voice. Alicia looked up to see a group of girls towering above her, their red-haired leader front and center. It was Samantha Whitlock, the girl from her gym class. Alicia collected her books from the ground and stood up.

"I don't have time for this, Samantha. What do you want?"

"Do I look like a joke to you?"

Alicia cracked a smile.

"Is that some trick question or something?"

"How would you like it if I punched you in the mouth?"

Alicia looked at her watch. She had five minutes to cross the campus to the next building.

"Look, I don't have time for this. I'm going to be late for class."

"Why were you laughing at me in gym class?"

Alicia remembered why she had laughed. Samantha was jumping rope when one of her feet became tangled, and she fell flat on her face. The whole thing would have elicited little laughter from any other student, but Samantha was a bully who picked on everyone – even boys. On more than one occasion, Alicia had seen her fight girls for trivial things like not saying hello to her or bumping her shoulder while passing in the hallway. So, when she fell, the whole gym laughed, and Alicia did too. Self-inflicted comeuppance was a rare comedy that everyone enjoyed.

"I wasn't laughing at you," lied Alicia as she looked past the group. "Look, I need to go."

"I saw you, bitch. Don't lie."

"Everyone was laughing," snapped Alicia. "Even these girls were."

Samantha moved closer.

"Maybe it's time someone taught you some manners."

Alicia placed her books on the floor. After gently placing her glasses on her books, she stood up to face Samantha.

"Look, you fat ugly-as-fuck, bitch! I tried to be nice, but now you're pushing me. If you don't want the whole damned school to see this little Black girl kick your fat ass up and down this hallway, I suggest you walk the fuck away."

Alicia's comments froze students in their tracks. The words were vulgar and confrontational to every student who heard them. It wasn't long before a large crowd was at the locker. Ignoring them, Alicia moved closer to Samantha with her fists clenched. Everyone could tell by the anger in her eyes that she was more significant than her size indicated.

"I will beat your motherfucking ass, bitch!" she growled.

Startled, Samantha took a step back with her mouth agape. Her friends stood befuddled as they searched each other's faces, unsure how to proceed. But there was no hesitation in Alicia. She meant every word she said. She smelled the fear coming from the group of girls, and it made her want to attack them like a rabid dog. In Alicia's mind, Samantha and her friends were nothing but a bunch of cowards, bullies trying to make themselves seem more significant at the expense of someone they perceived to be weak, the quiet little black girl. But Samantha and her friends had made a horrible mistake when they targeted Alicia. Although calm, she was less like a timid child and more like a hair trigger on a handgun; the slightest pressure could set her off. Alicia was a wolf in sheep's clothing. There was nothing she wanted more than to spill the blood of the whole group in the hallway.

After looking into Alicia's eyes for a few seconds, Samantha became frightened. She instantly searched for a way to exit the dangerous situation while saving face.

"You're lucky I don't have time to fight you. I have to get to class," Samantha mumbled while turning to walk away. But it was too late. Alicia's anger had boiled over. She grabbed a handful of Samantha's hair.

"Where do you think you're going, bitch?" she snapped. Before the girl could respond, Alicia yanked her hair so hard that she screamed.

"AAAAAH! Let go!"

But Alicia wanted blood. She yanked on the girl's hair again. This time, she pulled so hard that a loud pop sounded from the girl's neck.

"Ow! My neck!"

With fear in her eyes, Samantha looked to her friends for help. Instead, she got nothing. They all saw the bloodthirsty look on Alicia's face and took off running down the hall. Alicia grabbed another handful of Samantha's hair and hurled her face-first into the metal lockers. The sound of her face smashing against the metal made several of the students scream. Samantha fell to the floor with blood pouring from her mouth.

But Alicia didn't stop.

She climbed on top of the girl and pulled her hands away from her bloody face.

"You fat bitch! You fucked with the wrong one!" she growled.

The crowd watched in horror as she rained down blow after blow upon the girl's face. Soon, Samantha was unconscious.

"Stop!" yelled a girl from the crowd. Still, Alicia continued to strike Samantha's face. She smiled as she felt the bone in the girl's nose crack under her fist. She wanted Samantha to have a permanent reminder of her assault. No one would fuck with her after this.

Suddenly, a security guard emerged and tackled Alicia, sending them both sliding.

"Stop!" the officer yelled as he tried to smother her movement with his massive body.

"Get the fuck off of me, you prick!" she screamed.

Although he outweighed her by 100 pounds, the security guard struggled to contain Alicia. Her small hands moved swiftly beneath them as he held her down. Suddenly, she reached below his waist and smiled. The man screamed out in agony as Alicia squeezed hard on his testicles.

"Ow! Let go of my balls, you little bitch!"

"Go fuck your mother!"

Soon, a second security guard was on top of them.

"I got her, Jeff. Get up."

"I can't! The little bitch has my balls!"

The officer removed a long black flashlight from the loop on his belt and cracked Alicia twice on her shoulder. Alicia screamed out in pain as fire shot through her arm. She loosened her grasp, and the security guard rolled away, coughing while clutching his privates. The other officer flipped Alicia onto her belly.

"Just calm down," he said. "Take a deep breath. Relax. We're just going to visit the principal's office."

Suddenly, the hallway flooded with whistles and teachers. Students ran out of their classrooms to see the commotion. Alicia was carried off to the principal's office while the teachers attended to the bloody girl lying on the floor.

4

Power and Influence

Alicia sat in the waiting lounge outside the principal's office, handcuffed to a wooden bench. To her, being there was like sitting inside an ant community. She got to see the inner workings of the principal's office. Two middle-aged secretaries whirled around in front of her, answering phones and distributing handwritten passes to students arriving late to school. The secretaries also directed the maintenance men to various broken items needing attention. They received intercom messages from teachers who occasionally buzzed the office to inform the secretaries of disruptive students. The woman redirected sick students to the school nurse, and they also called Parents to question why a student had missed consecutive days of school.

And Alicia remained cuffed to the bench, waiting.

Occasionally, the handcuffs would make her hand go numb, and she had to twist her wrist to try to get the feeling back. Her knuckles hurt slightly from breaking Samantha's nose, and she rubbed it with her free hand. But beyond that, she didn't move or say anything.

Students were peering at her through the glass window; it didn't bother her. Neither did the looks she got from the secretaries; they looked at her like a criminal, an animal not fit to be amongst regular students. Whenever they looked over at her, Alicia smiled politely. In her mind, Samantha had gotten what she deserved. There was no reason for her to be sad about anything.

Suddenly, the Principal's office door opened, and a large woman walked out with the Principal in tow. Natalie was the same woman who had attempted to save her father from the confrontation at the grocery store when she was younger.

"Thank you, Mr. Canard. I appreciate your patience."

"We believe in second chances at Fletcher High School, Ms. Olsen. We want to be sure Ms. Kelly gets the attention she deserves. Diversion only works when there's active parental participation."

The principal nodded to the security guard standing just outside the door. The guard walked in and was about to unlock Alicia's arm from the bench when he paused.

"Watch your shit," he mumbled under his breath. Alicia smiled. It was the same officer she'd grabbed in the hallway.

"Watch your shit," she mumbled back. Startled, the security guard looked at her, grabbed her wrist, and squeezed. Finally, he unlocked her handcuffs and walked back into the hallway.

"Come on, Alicia. Let's go," said Natalie. Alicia got up and followed Natalie out of the building.

5

Explanations

"So, do you want to tell me what happened?"

Alicia leaned against the car window and watched the trees go by.

"Not really."

"Not really? What's going on with you, Alicia? You were doing so well."

Alicia kept quiet. Although Natalie meant well, sometimes talking with her was like talking to a police officer.

"So, why did you get into a fight with the girl?"

"What difference does it make?"

"What is that supposed to mean?"

Alicia rolled her eyes in frustration. The school was primarily white, and no matter what happened, she'd be the black girl with an "attitude" that would always get blamed.

"Okay. Do you want to know? They tried to bully me."

"They? The Principal told me it was one girl you fought with."

"You see?"

"See what?"

"I knew he wouldn't tell you everything. He probably told you I started the whole thing, right?"

"Well, he did say several people saw you hit the girl first."

"You see? He won't tell you that Samantha outweighs me by 100 pounds. He's not going to tell you that Samantha and her two friends showed up at my locker, threatening to beat me up because I laughed at her in gym class."

"Well, maybe he didn't tell me because he didn't know."

"I told him what happened! He just took her friends' word for it."

"Well, that's how the real world works, Alicia. Witnesses outweigh words."

Alicia turned away from Natalie.

"Dad was right. White folks must have different eyeballs than the rest of us. They see what they want to see."

"That's unfair."

"Try being a black girl and then talk to me about unfair."

"There are other ways to handle things, Alicia. You could've gotten a teacher involved."

"Or I could've gotten my ass kicked."

"I'm just saying. You have to be smarter than this."

"Look. I'm living in a mostly white town, attending a mostly white school with a white woman as a legal guardian. There is no smarter way. There's only the white way."

"Don't do that, Alicia. That's not fair. I'm trying to help. The fight could've easily ended up in court."

"And we both know you'll do anything to avoid that."

"What's that supposed to mean?"

Alicia ignored Natalie.

"You can ignore me if you want to, but this is the second school you've been to in a year. I can't keep pulling strings to protect you. If you don't control yourself, you'll do something I can't fix."

"Who asked you to protect me?"

"No one. I do it because I care about you."

"Care about me? That's a joke."

"Damn it, Alicia. Stop! I'm trying here. I'm trying."

The car pulled to the apartment complex, and Natalie turned off the engine. She took a deep breath and turned to face Alicia.

"You're suspended for two weeks. The girl has a broken nose and a fractured cheekbone. Luckily, her parents won't press charges."

"Let me guess, you paid them off?"

"Also, you're enrolled in Summer School."

"What?"

"Don't blame me, blame yourself. You transferred there mid-year, and now you're suspended for fighting. You have to catch up somehow. Summer School is the only answer. Otherwise, they're talking about holding you back a year."

"I'll bet this was all your doing, wasn't it?"

Natalie slapped the steering wheel in frustration.

"Damn it, how long are you going to keep this up?"

"Keep what up?"

"Don't make me say it."

"Say it. I don't give a fuck!"

"Don't curse at me, Alicia. You know what I mean. How long will you continue blaming the world for what happened?"

Alicia looked into Natalie's eyes.

"When will my dad be okay?"

"What?"

"When did the doctors say my dad will be okay?"

"Michael's injuries are permanent. You know that."

"Well, there you have it. That's the answer to your question." Alicia climbed out of the car, grabbed her backpack, and slammed the door. Natalie lowered the passenger window.

"Let's keep what happened between us. You know how Michael gets."

"Scared he might want to sue someone?"

"What?"

But Alicia ignored her and continued walking to the apartment building.

A frustrated Natalie restarted her car and drove away.

Alicia opened the door and walked into the dark apartment. After feeling around for the light switch, she turned it on.

"Daddy! I'm home!"

Alicia threw her books onto the sofa and headed to the TV room. When she walked in, that room was also dark. She flipped on the light switch.

"Daddy. Why do you have all the lights turned off? It's not healthy to sit in the dark."

She walked over to her dad sitting in the wheelchair, and kissed him.

"You're...home?" her father asked.

"Yes, Daddy. I'm home," Alicia responded.

Suddenly, Alicia gagged. The odor of urine and feces was strong in the apartment.

"Daddy. Did you soil yourself again?"

"I...tried to go....to...the bathroom...but..."

"But what, Daddy? If you can't go to the bathroom, I'll have to start buying diapers for you."

"F...fuck...diapers! I won't wear no...diapers! I'm a man! A man! I'm a...man!"

Alicia kissed her father's cheek.

"Okay, Daddy. You're a man. I know."

"N...no diapers...No...diapers...promise!"

"I promise, Daddy. No diapers. Okay? Don't worry. No Diapers. You're a man."

Alicia wheeled her dad into the bathroom. She pulled his pants and underwear down to his ankles and took them off. After wrapping both arms around her father, she lifted him and placed him on the toilet.

"There you go, Daddy. Try to use the bathroom. I'll start your bubble bath. You want a bubble bath, don't you?"

"Yeah... I like the bubble bath. Hot water is good for my legs."

Alicia turned on the hot water in the tub and poured the liquid into the bath.

"Go ahead and use the bathroom, Daddy. I'll go out back to clean the wheelchair. When I return, I'll put you in for your bath."

Alicia grabbed the hose and wheeled the chair out the apartment's back door. After spraying it down, she found a bucket and went into the kitchen to fill it with hot water, bleach, and soap. Alicia went back outside, grabbed the brush, and scrubbed the wheelchair all over until it was clean enough. After spraying the wheelchair, she dried it and pulled it back into the apartment. She returned to the bathroom to help her father.

"Okay, Daddy. Are you ready?"

"Yeah."

"Did you wipe yourself?"

"Yeah."

Once again, Alicia put both her arms around her dad. She winced as her face brushed against the deep indentation on his skull – even underneath his skin, she could feel the cold metal plate; it made his skin feel like a dead fish. Alicia spread her legs and lifted her dad onto the tub's edge. While holding him with one arm, she lifted his legs and swung them over the tub's edge into the water. Once his legs were in, she lifted him again and sat him in the water.

"Is the water okay, Daddy?"

"It's...good. Nice and warm."

"Okay. I'm going to get dinner ready. Make sure you wash everything, Daddy."

Suddenly, her father started laughing.

"No, do-do...stains."

Alicia started laughing.

"That's right. I don't have time to scrub your underwear. I need to do some homework."

As Alicia turned to walk out of the bathroom, her father yelled.

"Chuckles!"

"Yes, Daddy?"

"How...was...school?"

"It was okay. I learned a lot today."

"Yeah?"

"Yes, Daddy."

"Because you...know...you have to...be a doctor."

"I know, Daddy."

"So...you can...fix me."

Alicia turned away from her father when she heard those words. Although she knew he struggled, his words sometimes tugged at her soul. She wanted so much to reverse the horrible day that destroyed their lives. But there was no relief for the hell in which they lived. So, she just had to grin and bear it. She was her father's daughter. If he dared to endure the constant humiliations in front of his only child, she could handle giving him the love and support he needed.

"I'm going to get dinner started. I'll be back in a few minutes."

As she started preparing dinner for them, Alicia began to think about her mother. She couldn't help but wonder if things would've been different if her mother and father had stayed together. Alicia wondered where her mother was and what her mother was doing with her life. Did she have a new husband? Children? Did she know what had happened to the two of them? Alicia's father had told her that her mother was more concerned with partying and having a good time than being tied down with a family. Still, with things turning out the way they did, Alicia couldn't help but feel a great emptiness. Her mother would always be her mother, no matter her failed relationship with her father. And she shouldn't be absolved of those duties just because she didn't want them. Whether seen or unseen, Alicia still needed her mother.

After helping her father get dressed and after she'd finished cleaning the kitchen, Alicia went to her bedroom and flopped down on the bed. The day passed in such a whirl that she barely recalled it. Punching Samantha's face seemed like an old television show instead of something Alicia had done. She'd have to find something to do for her two-week suspension. Although her father wasn't as sharp as he once was, he was no fool. He'd ask questions if she sat around the house all day.

Alicia removed her shirt and sniffed under her arms. She didn't smell too bad. She was exhausted, but Alicia didn't have the energy to shower now. She'd shower in the morning. After removing her bra, she slid under the covers.

Alicia began combing over the day as she stared at the dark ceiling. Soon, her poor decision-making tumbled out at her from the darkness. Alicia heard Natalie's words in her head.

"...there are other ways to handle things, Alicia."

Alicia lifted her pillow from the bed and smashed it on her face.

"Idiot. Easier said when you have everything."

Her mind flashed back to the incident with the police. She remembered Natalie being the first to reach into the hot car to rescue the tiny girl trembling in the backseat. Alicia remembered how Natalie had sat with her in the hospital. While the doctors worked on Alicia's dad, Alicia and Natalie played with little dolls, anything to keep her mind off of what was happening behind the big metal doors. She remembered how Natalie had temporarily moved into the apartment with them and cooked, cleaned, and cried – all while helping her father regain his strength.

But it wasn't long before Alicia discovered why Natalie had given so much time, energy, and money to help them. One night, as she lay in bed, she heard whispers. She climbed out of bed and cracked her door to listen. Natalie was talking to her dad.

"It'll be easier for everyone. You'll see. You will still be Alicia's dad. I'll be a primary contact to make decisions about Alicia's future," whispered Natalie.

"I don't know... she's my...daughter," replied her father.

"She needs attention that you can't give her, Michael. She's a little girl. She needs to be around someone who can teach her the proper way. Don't you want that?"

"Yeah...I think so...maybe."

"Then it's settled. I'll have the attorney draw up the papers."

"And Alicia...won't leave me?"

"No. Things won't change much. This arrangement is only for her schooling needs."

But everything did change. In time, Natalie moved in permanently and became hostile towards Alicia's dad. Although she was a child, Alicia could tell that most of Natalie's frustration was laziness. Natalie was obese and verbally protested whenever Alicia's father needed help. Natalie's hostility towards Alicia's father became more prominent as time passed. She'd do things like not bathe him for multiple days. Sometimes, her dad would smell so bad that when Alicia came home from school, she would have to take off her dad's clothing and spray him with the hose behind the apartment. It hurt her so much when her father would cry because of the ice-cold water, but she didn't have a choice. She couldn't lift him into the tub.

Alicia also noticed a duality in Natalie's personality that she hadn't seen before. Natalie's loneliness dominated her thoughts. She told Alicia of the numerous times her boyfriends had abandoned her. There was a tone of pity to it all as if she was attempting to gain sympathy. She hated men, yet she would do anything to have one. She believed that all men were jerks, but every woman needed a man to feel complete. She was the unluckiest woman on earth and cried over not having a baby. Yet she was so happy to be alone and free of "stretch marks."

Natalie was also vocal about her financial contributions to their survival. Whenever she didn't like something, she'd complain about "all that she's done" and how ungrateful "some people" were for having someone to pay the bills. It wasn't long before even her dad told her to stop complaining.

"No...one...asked you to...be here," he'd say when he could take no more. Angry and unable to attack the man without a full-blown fight from Alicia, Natalie would usually leave the apartment and go on a drive. Hours later, she'd return with a peace offering (ice cream or cake) and pretend the incident never happened.

Things continued like this for months before an incident that pushed Natalie out of their apartment to live independently. Alicia had just gotten off her school bus and was attempting to unlock the front door when she heard raised voices.

"YOU! YOU! YOU!" her father yelled.

"I don't have to take this shit from you, Michael! I can leave!"

"WHY DIDN'T YOU...TELL ME? WHY? YOU! YOU! YOU!"

Alicia ran to her father and tried to calm him. She couldn't understand what had upset him so. Alicia's father had knocked a vase off the table and was thrashing about in his wheelchair. Alicia kissed his face and tried to comfort him.

"Daddy. Shhhh. I'm here, Daddy. It's me. Calm down."

Unable to calm him, Alicia ran to Natalie.

"What happened? Why is Daddy so upset?"

"Go figure. I'm tired of this shit! I don't need this."

"Why is he yelling?"

"I don't know. Michael has it in his head that I'm here to protect my family."

"What? I don't understand."

"Talk to him. I'm going to pack up my stuff and leave. I don't need this shit."

Natalie packed her bags and left that same day. After she was gone, Alicia calmed her father long enough to get the truth. Alicia's father asked Natalie why she didn't allow him to see an attorney because of his injuries. Natalie became angry. Soon, she was naming how she had helped Alicia and her father. Sensing that she seemed more concerned with protecting her family than doing what was right, Alicia's father exploded. He told Natalie to leave his apartment and that he wouldn't accept any help from her again.

At first, Alicia panicked. She was a kid. How could Alicia take care of herself and her dad? She struggled to cook, clean the house, and care for her father for weeks. Eventually, Natalie reached out to her. Although Alicia's father forbade Natalie from entering their home again,

Natalie continued interacting with Alicia. She taught her how to care for her dad. Natalie sent a nurse to help with his baths. She gave Alicia books to read. Natalie taught her what to do when Alicia's period came. But things were never the same after she moved out. Alicia realized that her father had been right. It was evident that Natalie didn't want to take care of her dad. Why not just allow them to go to court? Alicia and her dad would get what was rightfully theirs, and everyone could move on.

Alicia accepted Natalie's help, but she didn't trust her. How could she? Although injured, her father wasn't stupid, and Alicia agreed. From how Natalie behaved, Alicia began to think that everything had been a way to minimize the impact of a lawsuit against Natalie's family. What better way to have a case dropped than to take control of someone's child? Besides, Natalie didn't even like children, especially ones that were old enough to think for themselves. She complained whenever she had to do anything other than lift a fork to her mouth. And Alicia was supposed to believe that her heart was so big that she would be willing to give up a life of laziness for an injured man and his motherless daughter? Given all that had happened, Natalie had to know that eventually, the teenager would figure it out. She was only searching for the right time to leave.

Her eyelids became heavy as Alicia lay in bed, thinking about everything. Soon, fatigue made her thoughts heavy. Slowly, Alicia fell asleep.

6 |

Julian's High School Days

The bell rang, and the students flooded out of their classrooms into the hallway. Julian ran out of his classroom and through the doors leading to the breezeway. Once outside, he sat on the edge of the brick wall, staring at the double doors. He only had to wait a few minutes before he saw Amisha exit the building. As soon as she saw him, Amisha lowered her head and tried to walk past him quickly.

"Amisha! Wait!"

"I can't talk right now. I need to get to class."

"Come on, just give me 5 minutes. Please."

Reluctantly, Amisha stopped walking and turned to face Julian.

"What is it? Hurry up. I need to go."

"We haven't talked since your parents came back. I just wanted to make sure everything is okay."

Amisha rolled her eyes and looked at her watch.

"Look, I've got to go."

"Wait. I know you're mad. I just wanted to explain what happened."

"What are you, on drugs or something?"

"No, it's nothing like that."

"Are you gay?"

"What? Of course not!"

Amisha lowered her voice as a group of students walked by.

"Then explain yourself. My parents left town for a full week, and you spent the night at my house every night! We slept naked in the same bed, and we still didn't do it! For seven days?! How is that normal?"

"There's something I need to tell you. Something that happened."

"What's going on, Julian? People our age are supposed to be fucking their brains out."

"I know. I know."

"What is it? Don't you find me attractive?"

"Of course! You're the most beautiful girl in the world to me!"

"Were you afraid I'd get pregnant? I'm on the pill, and I brought condoms. It couldn't have been that. You couldn't even get hard. Either you're gay, or I'm not attractive to you. Which is it?"

"Look. Let's meet this evening, and I promise to tell you everything."

Amisha ignored him.

"And the two days we did make out? Weird."

"Lower your voice."

"I mean, you want me to choke you and hit you while you kiss me down there? You wanted me to spit on you and call you names? What the fuck!"

Suddenly, Amisha's friend walked by with her boyfriend.

"Ooooh. It looks like someone is in trouble," said the girl as they passed. Amisha and Julian flashed uncomfortable smiles until the two were out of sight.

"I want to tell you later. Can we please meet at the coffee shop?"

"Not today. I have cheerleading practice."

"Then, when?"

"Maybe tomorrow."

"Okay."

"And you'd better tell me everything. I don't know how much longer I can deal with this."

Julian started getting nervous.

"You didn't tell anyone, did you?"

"No. I haven't. But my friends have been asking why we haven't fucked. I can't keep lying about this. Either tell me what's going on, or I'm leaving. I can't keep doing this."

As Amisha walked away, Julian shook his head in disappointment. Although he liked her, he knew they couldn't be together. There was no way she would accept who Julian was or his past. Julian wasn't sure he would share his history with anyone, let alone a 17-year-old high school cheerleader. Julian's memories were a fog of facts and lies that his mind had trouble separating. There was no doubt in his mind that he needed help. But needing help and asking for it were two different things. Who knew why his mind craved the abuse of his past? He indeed didn't. He regretted displaying who he was to Amisha. Why had he done that? What the hell was he thinking? Emotionally, Amisha was a stranger to him. Other than knowing her favorite color, he knew none of her secrets. And now she knew – at least partially – his darkest desires.

Julian took a deep breath and put on his backpack. After talking with Amisha, one thing had become clear to him: Amisha would undoubtedly tell her friends about their nights in her parents' house. There was only one way he could protect himself from her gossiping friends – and it wouldn't be pretty.

At 6:00 pm, the high school locker room flooded with sweaty boys coming in from the football field. The practice was over, yet the yelling and screaming seemed to intensify. Soon, the sound of lockers banging filled the room, and athletic equipment flew through the air as the teenagers discussed practice and their prospects for the upcoming tournament.

"Man! Did you see the way Julian hit me with that pass? Right on the money! There's no way we won't win the tournament this year. No way!" yelled Kevin.

"All I know is when we play Middleburg, we're going to look good for the scouts in the stands," replied Julian as he took off his shoulder pads.

"We'll crush Middleburg this year," exclaimed Michael, the overweight center who could barely remove any of his equipment without help. "Hey Kevin, give me a hand with these pads?" Kevin stood up on the bench and pulled up on Michael's shoulder pads.

"Damn, Michael! You need to go on a diet!"

"And if I do that, who will keep Julian safe in the pocket?"

"Yeah, Kevin. Leave Mike alone. He's got a big workload."

"He could stand to lose one or two pounds. That's all I'm saying."

Suddenly, a nude player walked past Kevin into the showers.

"Did y'all see those cheerleaders practicing on the track next to us?"

Suddenly, testosterone filled the locker room as each boy contributed to the conversation.

"Did I? Those girls were hot!"

"Seriously hot! Especially the head cheerleader. What's her name? Brenda?"

"Tits for days, let me tell you. I'd bang that."

"Your ugly ass couldn't bang a hole in a tree!"

The group of football players burst into laughter at the joke.

"Truthfully, Julian is the only guy hitting anything over there!"

"What? For real?"

"Which one?"

"He's dating Amisha. I think that's her name. Amisha."

"How long have you been keeping that one under wraps?"

Julian opened his locker to evade some of the attention.

"We've been dating for about six months," he confessed.

His answer set off howling and hooping amongst the boys.

"6 months? Are you getting married?"

"Not."

"Not? What does that mean?"

"I can't talk about it."

"Aw, come on. What's the matter? Does her dad hate you?"

"The sex is bad? What is it?"

Julian lowered his voice.

"If I were to tell you guys, you wouldn't even believe me."

A restrained hush fell over the group of boys nearest to Julian.

"What is it, dude? Come on, you can tell us."

Julian shook his head and grabbed a towel for the shower.

"It's strange."

Now, every boy in the locker room pushed towards Julian's locker, hanging onto his words.

"What is it?" asked Kevin.

"She's a freak," Julian responded.

"What?" the group asked at once.

"What does that mean?"

"A freak like, how?"

Julian took a breath and then let it go.

"She's into weird shit. She wanted me to choke her. Call her names. You know, verbally abuse her."

The group let out a collective gasp.

"For real?"

"Seriously?"

Julian continued.

"No joke. I tried to have sex with Amisha, but she only wanted to give me a BJ."

"No way!"

"Real sick shit. Amisha wanted me to spit on her and slap her face while she blew me."

"No fucking way!" exclaimed Kevin.

"Y'all can have her if you want her. That chick is nuts."

Julian dropped his briefs and headed to the shower. Before entering, he turned to look at the group of boys standing with their mouths open. Julian turned on the hot shower and put his head in the water. His relationship with Amisha was officially over. But he didn't have a choice. It was either her or him. And seeing as how he was the football team's quarterback, his word carried more weight than hers. It was the only play he could make.

When Julian came out of the shower, someone threw a towel and hit him in the face.

"Hey, Julian. Coach wants to see you in his office," said Kevin.

Julian went to his locker and got dressed. Afterward, he walked into the coach's office.

"Coach? You wanted to see me?"

"Take a seat, Julian."

Julian sat on the old torn loveseat in front of the coach's desk.

"You memorize those new plays yet?"

"Not yet, Coach. But I'm working on it."

"We need you to be sharp for next week's game. That's when we will test run a few new plays for the tournament."

Julian shook his head in agreement. Coach Jeffries was tough on his players when it came to learning. Whether it was a playbook strategy or in the classroom, the coach expected sharp memories and perfect execution. His coaching style was old school, and everyone admired him for it. At the games, Parents marveled at the older man with the scruffy gray beard marching up and down the field, yelling instructions to the players. Julian felt close to Coach Jeffries. Out of all the people in his life, Coach was the only one that acted like he genuinely gave a damn.

"Look, Julian. I called you in here because I've received feedback from your teachers."

Julian sat up in the chair. Based on his grades, he knew what was coming. Coach Jeffries reached into his desk and pulled out a thick folder.

"Most of your teachers say you're doing a good job. But several of them think you could benefit from some extra studying."

"What?"

"Math. Your Algebra teacher says you're having quite a bit of difficulty."

"Well, I can't lie, coach. I hate math."

"Hate it or not, what you're doing isn't working."

"I'm trying my best, Coach."

"So, maybe you need some help."

"You mean a tutor?"

"No. I looked at your grades. I think we're past tutoring."

"So, what do you suggest, coach?"

"You're going to have to give up a few weeks of your summer for summer school."

Julian was shocked.

"What about the summer practice with the team?"

"We'll pull you out on the last two weeks of summer to get you back into shape."

Coach Jeffries walked from around his desk and slapped Julian on the back.

"I know it's not what you want to hear, but there's no other way. You're entering your senior year next year. And rather than waiting until all the red lights are flashing, it's better we go ahead and get a jump on things. I have big plans for you."

Julian looked up at his coach.

"Plans?"

"Next year, you'll be the star on that football field. All kinds of scouts will be coming here to look at you."

"Really?"

"If you play your cards right, you can go to any college you want on a free ride. But none of that will happen if you can't do the bookwork. I give all my players' teachers specific instructions to give them extra work. Nobody gets to slouch in class. And you're not the exception."

Julian stood up and threw his bag over his shoulder. He knew there was no point in trying to negotiate with Coach Jeffries. What he said was gospel.

"So, get yourself ready for Summer School. We only have a short time to prepare you for college."

"Okay. Thanks, Coach."

Coach Jeffries smiled at Julian.

"On your way out, tell Taylor to come in."

Julian walked out of the office and did as instructed. Afterward, he went home.

7

Home Life

Julian unlocked the door and walked into the house. The thick, suffocating aroma of marijuana hit him in the face like a ton of bricks. He hated it when his Uncle smoked it in the house. It made the whole place smell like cat piss.

"Lock that door behind you," his Uncle Dexter yelled from the dining room table. Julian turned around and locked the door.

"Damn, College Boy! That's a big ass bookbag," exclaimed one of the men sitting at the table. "What are you studying to be, a lawyer?"

"Damn, Dexter. Do you live with a goddamned college boy? Why the fuck are you so dumb?"

The table of men burst out laughing.

Julian walked past the men at the table and down the hallway to his room.

"There are some chicken wings on the stove if you want it," said Dexter.

"That's alright. I'll eat something later."

"What's the matter, the schoolboy is too good to eat with us?" asked one of the men while taking a deep puff on the marijuana-filled cigar shared around the table.

"Leave him alone. That's my sister's boy. He's doing big things in school," replied Dexter.

"Go ahead and knock out that homework, young buck," he continued as Julian closed the door to his bedroom.

Julian twisted his face in disgust. His Uncle always liked to pretend that he was a good Uncle to his friends, but he was a piece of shit. The chicken wings his Uncle had offered Julian were Julian's, not his Uncle's. He'd purchased them two days ago. There was hardly any food in the house, and when there was, it was because Julian had bought it with the money he'd earned working weekends at Mike's Seafood Shack. In Julian's mind, his Uncle Dexter was nothing but a bullshit artist.

Once his bedroom door was closed, Julian immediately walked over to his dresser and opened his sock drawer. He pushed aside a few socks, searching for the money he'd placed there before he went to school. It was gone.

"Fuck!" he cursed as he slammed the sock drawer closed. He'd saved that money for his mom. Now, he'd have to find a way to earn it back before visiting his mother in prison in the morning. Frustrated, Julian turned out his lights and fell on his bed. As he stared into the darkness, he listened to his Uncle entertaining his other loser friends. He heard them joking about which girl had the fattest ass and which lowlife owed money to who. They discussed politics as if they voted and argued over which boxer would win the championship. There were discussions about who had the best dime bag of weed and who had hit the "numbers." None of the men seemed to care that a teenager was within earshot of their highly inappropriate conversations.

Julian sat up on his bed and pulled his curtains open. The streetlight just outside his window bathed the room in a dirty yellow light. At that moment, a massive burst of laughter from the inconsiderate men at the table pushed into the room. Julian turned to look at his empty dresser. It was moments like this that he wished he still had his boombox. But his Uncle had pawned it. He'd claimed that someone broke into the apartment and took it, but when Julian entered the pawnshop, he saw it on sale in the window.

Julian hated his Uncle. Although he'd been with him through his mother's arrest, Uncle Dexter turned out to be the worst person his mother could've chosen to look out for her son. On top of being addicted to alcohol, his Uncle Dexter had an even stronger addiction to gambling. If payments for the apartment hadn't been taken out of his welfare check and paid directly to the office, Julian was sure they would've been on the street long ago. In many ways, Julian felt as though he were the parent working a part-time job to keep them both from starving to death.

Soon, the noise from the men transformed into white noise. Not long after closing his eyes, Julian fell asleep.

8

Locked Away

Julian woke up before sunrise the next day to prepare for his trip. After showering and brushing his teeth, he went to the kitchen to grab something to eat. After remembering that the refrigerator was empty, he snatched the two dried chicken wings from the pan on the stove. Julian shoved a dry chicken wing into his mouth and ran out the door. He had to make it to the D-12 bus stop before it became too crowded; whoever was last to get on the bus would probably end up standing up the entire trip until they reached downtown. As soon as he arrived at the bus stop, Julian breathed a sigh of relief. Only two Hispanic ladies were sitting on the bench, waiting for the bus to arrive. Seconds later, the bus pulled up to the stop and opened its doors.

When the bus finally reached the terminal, the sun had come up, and the line for ticket purchasing was long. Julian was happy he'd purchased his ticket a week earlier. He began to pace in front of the small building as he waited for the bus to arrive. Whenever visiting his mother in prison, Julian became so excited that it was difficult to control himself. The trips always felt like he was on a stage to audition for a talent show. Although they didn't live under the same roof, she loomed large in his life. She had a way of seeing what was going on with him without even being in the same house. She could tell if he was having problems with schoolwork based on his response to her questions. She could tell if his Uncle Dexter, her brother, gave Julian a hard time and would seek to reach out to her brother to rectify the issue as best she could. She was as motherly as one could expect. Living in a jail cell miles away from a son had a way of impacting parental abilities. But even though she wasn't around, Julian still respected his mother. He not only respected her word, but he also craved it. Jail couldn't change the fact that his mother was his mother.

Within a few moments, the bus arrived. Julian boarded the bus and found an available window seat. As he watched the other riders climb on board, Julian wondered if he should tell his mother that her brother had stolen the money he'd saved. He decided against it. His mother had enough going on in her life. She couldn't mediate fights between her brother and her son.

Julian reached into his back pocket and pulled out a photo of his mother. With his thumb, he rubbed his mom's face and smiled. She was a much younger woman back then. Her natural beauty, curly hair, and dazzling smile warmed him. He missed her immensely; the smell of her hair when she kissed him goodnight, the silly way his mother used to dance throughout the apartment as she cleaned; the loud snores coming from her bedroom after she'd put in a long shift at work. Julian missed her so much—the trips to see her rejuvenated his soul. Without the visits, he seriously doubted he'd be able to navigate life.

Finally, everyone was on the bus, and the driver left the terminal. Julian closed his eyes and tried to relax. In four hours, he'd be with his mom again.

9

What a Mother Knows

"**Y**ou look thin, boy. Why haven't you been eating?" asked Julian's mother as she looked at him from the other side of the table.

"I've been eating," Julian lied. "Coach Jeffries has been working hard to prepare us for this tournament."

Julian's mother reached out and touched his face.

"You're looking more and more like your father," she said. Suddenly, a guard yelled from a few feet away.

"No physical contact, sir!"

The warning annoyed Julian's mother, and she let it be known.

"Alright. Alright. Don't get your drawers in a bunch," Julian's mother replied.

Julian instinctively tried to change the conversation. The correctional officers could make things difficult for their visits if they deemed his mother's behavior belligerent.

"Hey, Mom, I'll deposit money to your commissary on Friday next week."

"No worries, honey. I have more than enough to hold me over."

Julian leaned back in his chair and looked at his mom. Prison had changed her, and she barely resembled the woman in the photo. Her eyes were veiny and red. Her lips were chapped and had dark spots on them from smoking cigarettes. She no longer tried to "do" her hair. Instead, she sported long, thick corn rolls stretching from her head's front to the back. The orange jumpsuit she wore almost wholly stripped away any appearance of femininity. Instead, what remained was a woman who looked more and more criminal to Julian with every visit.

"You're up for parole soon, aren't you?"

"Next year."

"You ready?"

"Am I ready? What kind of question is that? Of course, I'm ready. I'm ready to get back to you."

"It'll be so good to have you home."

"Let's take it day by day. We still have a long time. Anyway, how's school?"

"Okay."

"Aw shit. What's going on? Give it to me."

"It's nothing much. The coach said I needed to go ahead with summer school."

"Why? You've been skipping out on your homework?"

"No, mom. It's nothing like that. But Algebra is kicking my butt. I'm falling far behind."

"Well, you need to focus more. You'll probably need to give up something if you can't straighten it. Working or maybe even football."

Julian acknowledged his mother's words by nodding his head. He didn't know how to explain his financial situation to her without setting off alarm bells. How could he explain that if he stopped working, he wouldn't be able to eat? Not to mention how his unemployment would cripple his ability to send money to her commissary prison account.

"How's that girlfriend of yours? What was her name? Amisha?"

"Yeah. Amisha."

"So? How's it going?"

"Not too good, Mom."

Julian's mother looked surprised.

"Really? What happened?"

"It's complicated."

"Well, judging from how you're juggling school, sports, and work, it was only a matter of time before those struggles crept over to your girl-friend. What is it? Is she complaining about time?"

"Not exactly."

"Look, Julian. Either you put in the work, or you need to leave it alone. She's a woman. And one thing we women refuse to tolerate is ne-glect."

"It's not that, mom."

Julian lowered his head and took a deep breath. No matter how close he and his mother were, he couldn't tell her about the sexual difficulties he was having. His mother stared at him for a few seconds before con-tinuing.

"You still have those bad dreams? You know. About Dori?"

"Mom, please. Can we not talk about that?"

Julian hated talking about the past with his mother. Although he knew she meant well, the past smothered him so much that he struggled to contain the pain he still felt inside.

"Amisha and I broke up, Mom. And it had nothing to do with Ms. Hicks, Okay?"

"Uh-huh. Sure. Whatever you say."

"It doesn't."

"You know I don't believe you, right?"

"Believe it or not, it's over. Ms. Hicks had nothing..."

"Why do you keep calling that bitch Ms. Hicks? It's like she's worthy of respect or something. Her name was Dori. A fucking pedophile. Stop calling her Miss, okay?"

Julian watched as his mother worked herself up into a frenzy of frus-tration. She made a fist and pounded it against her forehead repeatedly.

"Mom. Please calm down. Can we talk about something else?"

"I swear to God. I'm not sorry about stabbing that bitch. If I could do it all again, I would."

"Mom! Don't say that!"

"Look at you! She took so much from you! From us! She's been dead for years, and what she did is still sapping the happiness out of our lives."

"It's over, mom."

"I'm glad that fucking bitch is dead. I know killing is wrong, but every night when I lay in that dark cell, I always get a little comfort knowing she can't hurt another family as she did ours."

"Mom, you can't think that way. When you go before the parole board, they can tell if you're remorseful for what you've done."

Julian's mother snapped.

"I don't give a fuck! Fuck that bitch! I'm glad she's fucking dead!"

The security guard looked over at Julian's mother as she angrily slammed her fists on the table.

"Excuse me, Christina. Is there a problem?" asked the guard.

"No, there isn't, Officer Davis. Why don't you go back to your corner and leave us the fuck alone?" Christina responded.

"That's it. Stand up," said the officer, pulling handcuffs from his waist. "Visit over."

Julian interrupted.

"But we still have 30 minutes."

"Blame your mom for spoiling that. Return in a few weeks when she's simmered down a bit."

Christina winced as he tightened the cuffs on her wrists.

"Fuck you for this, Officer Davis. You got to put cuffs on a mother in front of her kid?"

"Don't blame me. You know the rules. Visitation over."

Christina turned to face Julian.

"Don't worry, baby. Come back in a couple of weeks, and everything will be okay. We'll finish our conversation then."

Julian stood and watched as the officer led his mother out of the room until she was gone. He hadn't noticed everyone visiting with their loved ones staring at him to see what he would do next. Embarrassed and disappointed, Julian exited the building to catch the bus home.

10

Julian's First Day of Summer

Julian rolled over and looked at the alarm clock. Although he still had a few minutes before the alarm went off, he climbed out of bed and turned it off. He wished there was a select button he could press to speed through summer. It was Julian's first time relinquishing his summer to book study, and it felt like a prison. While Julian was in class, other students would probably be out gallivanting through the city, enjoying their summer. Frustrated with what he would miss out on, Julian took a shower.

When Julian came out of the shower, he heard the telephone in his bedroom ringing. After quickly wiping the water off his body, he grabbed the receiver and answered.

"Hello?"

"You son of a bitch!"

"Who is this?"

But Julian knew who it was. It was Amisha. He knew he would be getting a call from her, but Julian didn't know when he'd be receiving it.

"You know who it is, you piece of shit!"

Although it was early morning, Julian could tell from her voice that Amisha had been crying.

"What is it?"

"How could you?"

Julian heard a ruffling on the phone receiver. He knew someone else was listening. He figured it was either one of her friends or someone helping her seek revenge.

"How could I what?"

"You know the lies you told about me!"

"Lies? I don't know what you're talking about."

"What kind of person does that? I never hurt you! I never told any-one about the weird shit you were into."

"Amisha, you're not making sense right now. I have no idea what you're talking about."

"Julian? Are you going to do this? You know you started this rumor about me."

"Look, I don't have time for this right now. I'll talk to you later, Amisha."

Julian hung up the phone and sat down on his bed. He felt terrible about what he'd done to Amisha, but he had no choice. Maybe she would've been less vocal about spreading the rumor than he had been, but there was no doubt in his mind that she would've revealed his secret.

After thinking about things for a few more minutes, Julian finished getting dressed. Minutes later, he headed out the door to Summer School.

11

Alicia's First Day of Summer

Alicia couldn't remember when she started shoplifting; she estimated that she began shoplifting when Natalie stopped living with them, close to when Alicia got expelled. At first, she began stealing out of necessity to get the things she and her father needed without asking Natalie for a handout. In the beginning, the words of her father caused her to hesitate. She could hear the words he'd said to her in the car on the day the police attacked him:

"Taking something without paying for it is stealing."

Sometimes, those words would shut her down while shoplifting, forcing her to put whatever item she'd planned to take back on the shelf. But in time, her desire to take things became overwhelming, and she couldn't help herself. Alicia told herself she was getting back at "the man" for what the system had done to Alicia and her father. She romanticized the act by limiting herself to only taking things they "needed." But after a while, she realized she just liked "stealing shit." She took the things they needed and the things they didn't. She stole steaks and medicine. She took clothing and books. She couldn't describe the sensation of taking things under people's noses. Alicia remembered when she took a padlock from a hardware store while the security guard was "supposedly" watching her the whole time. She didn't need the lock. Alicia just wanted to try to get away with doing it. As soon as she left the store, she threw the item in the garbage. She only did it to see how good she was.

So, on her first day of Summer School, Alicia stopped at the convenience store down the street from her school, intending to steal something. She entered the building and walked to the rear. As she walked down the aisle, she passed numerous students; they stood in groups in front of the racks of candy and snacks. Alicia breathed a sigh of relief. Although the store had one roaming security guard, there would be no way he would track all the loud students throughout the store.

Alicia walked up to the magazine case to grab her favorite magazine. Another student was standing there reading a book. As if the boy didn't exist, she coolly reached around the teenager and grabbed a magazine. Without giving it a second thought, she put the magazine into her purse. The boy turned and looked at Alicia briefly. He placed the magazine back on the shelf and moved to the candy rack where the other students were. Once again, as if his presence was irrelevant, Alicia continued shopping by reaching around him to grab a candy bar and two bags of chips. The boy stood marveling at her courage. Alicia shoved all the items into her purse and walked to the front of the store. Finally, the boy grabbed a candy bar and went to the counter to pay for it.

After paying for his candy bar, the boy looked at Alicia as she passed in front of the security guard to exit the building.

"Ms., I'm going to need you to open your purse," the guard said. Alicia looked confused. It was only the second time since she'd been shoplifting that someone had requested to look in her bag.

"What?" she asked. "Open my purse? For what?"

The security guard's young face made Alicia feel she could either outsmart him or overpower his demands.

"What is this, a summer job for you?" she snapped. But the young security guard stood his ground.

"Either you open your purse, or I'll ban you from entering the store for one year."

"Why? Because I don't want to show you the maxi-pads inside? You're an idiot."

The lady ringing up the customers walked over to the security guard.

"Is there a problem?"

"Yes, she doesn't want to open her purse."

Feeling that the woman would be more compassionate in her attempt to escape, Alicia tried to appeal to her feminine side.

"I tried to explain to this guy that I didn't want to open my purse to expose the world to the fact that it's my time of the month."

The security looked away from the two women as they talked.

"Okay. Would you feel better if you stepped over beside the cash register and opened your purse for me?"

"Not really. I mean, why am I being singled out?"

Alicia was starting to panic. She hadn't anticipated another woman could neutralize her defenses.

"I assure you that's not the case, okay? We do this regularly with all the high school students up the street."

"But you're not asking to see inside a backpack. You're asking to see inside my purse. It's different."

The cashier shook her head. Alicia could tell she was losing patience.

"It's as the security guard just told you. Open your purse, or we must ban you from the store for one year."

Alicia was about to cut her losses and leave the store when something surprising happened. The boy who had witnessed Alicia's shoplifting walked up to the cashier and whispered in the cashier's ear. The woman jumped in surprise and immediately walked over to the security guard. The guard stood up and walked quickly towards the group of students in the rear of the store. Seconds later, the boy pulled Alicia out of the door.

"What's happening?" she asked the boy as he quickly walked away from the store.

"Go. Don't stop," the boy replied as he and Alicia walked away. Quickly, Alicia looked over her shoulder back at the store. She could see people exiting the building.

"What did you tell them?"

"It's better if you don't know."

As Alicia and the boy crossed the road, the boy took off running.

"Hey!" Alicia yelled after him. But he was so far ahead of her in seconds that she didn't bother. Alicia was soon at the entrance to the school. She paused to contemplate what had just happened. Finally, the bell rang, and she went inside.

12

Alicia Meets Julian

Alicia didn't know what to expect when entering her high school. When Natalie told her she would have to attend Summer School, she imagined one large classroom sitting on the football field's edge with a substitute teacher playing overseer to uncontrollable kids. Instead, what Alicia encountered was the same as regular school days. Before arriving at school, she received a letter indicating who her "homeroom" teacher would be and that she needed to be seated in that teacher's classroom before the 8:30 am bell rang. Once there, the teacher took attendance and let the students congregate until the second bell rang to report to their assigned classes. There were seven learning periods and seven different courses each student had to attend before the day ended.

The thing most surprising to Alicia about Summer School was the amount of "regular kids" attending. Sure, there were the normal troublemakers who made a ruckus during regular school, but there were also people that Alicia would never suspect of needing to attend. For example, the quiet girl sat in the back of Alicia's Algebra class. She always turned her homework in on time and never missed class. When the teacher asked her a question, she participated. Alicia couldn't believe that she got roped into Summer School. And then there was the most popular girl in school, Grace Matthews. All the guys wanted to date her, and every girl wanted to be her friend. With her thousand-watt smile and skill at working any room, who would've thought Grace wasn't academically knocking it out of the park?

Alicia's first class was English with Mrs. Sheppard. Her classroom was close to Alicia's homeroom, so she didn't have difficulty finding it. She walked into the room and went to the empty desks at the back. After sliding herself into the desk nearest the window and removing her books from her backpack, Alicia watched the students enter the classroom. As the sunshine warmed her desk, she wondered how she could endure three months in school while the rest of the world was enjoying summer. Suddenly, the late bell sounded, and the teacher rose from her desk.

"Okay, do we have everyone?" the elderly silver-haired woman asked. She walked to the door and was about to close it when a student rushed through. Alicia was shocked. It was the guy from the convenience store!

The tall black teenager paused beside Mrs. Sheppard and searched the room for an open desk.

"Getting here on time usually prevents awkward situations like this," snapped the teacher as she pointed in Alicia's direction. "There's a desk in the rear of the classroom. Go to the back and take a seat."

Julian took a few steps between the desks before his eyes locked on the girl beside the empty seat. It was the girl from the convenience store.

"Is anyone sitting here?" he asked Alicia.

"No," she responded without looking at him. Julian slid into the seat and made himself comfortable. Soon, the teacher started taking attendance. She called various names, and each student replied in the same half-dead response. When the teacher called Julian's name, he responded like all the other students. Still, his deep voice startled Alicia when he spoke, and she turned to look at him. Before Julian made eye contact, Alicia looked down at her book.

The rest of the class breezed by without Julian and Alicia even looking at one another. The summer heat warmed the classroom and left most of the students comatose as the dull hum of the teacher's voice lulled everyone into a trance. Julian and Alicia exited the classroom with the other students when the bell rang.

Julian ran out of the classroom and down the hall. His next class was in the other building. If he got there fast enough, he might be able to sit outside and eat his candy bar before going in. As he burst through the double doors, two hands grabbed the front of his shirt and pulled him to the side of the building. Julian struggled to maintain his balance and quickly looked to his right to see who'd grabbed him. It was a man that seemed too old to be a high school student. His face had a ragged, un-kempt beard that had spots of gray within it. Julian had never seen the man before.

"What the fuck?" Julian asked as he stuck out his hands to break his fall before he hit the sidewalk. He felt a kick to his ribs as he fell on his stomach. He looked up to see a much younger boy standing to his left. The older man who had grabbed him lifted Julian from the ground and threw him against the building.

"You're the motherfucker that talked shit about Amisha, aren't you?"

Pain shot through Julian's side, and he grabbed his ribs.

"What are you talking about?"

"Amisha, you bitch! She told us that you started rumors about her."

"Look, man, I don't know what she told you, but you got it wrong."

The teenager who kicked Julian in the side punched him in the stom-ach, and Julian doubled over in pain.

"You trying to call my cousin a liar, motherfucker?"

The older man grabbed Julian by his throat and lifted him off the ground. Julian gasped as he struggled to take in air. Suddenly, the door opened beside him, and Alicia walked out. As she walked past the three men grappling on the side of the exit, Julian let out a loud gurgling noise to get her attention. Alicia paused and turned around to look at the three men. Unable to talk, Julian mouthed the words,

"Get help."

Alicia walked closer to the men and stopped.

"What the fuck do you want bitch?" snapped the older man as he continued choking Julian.

"Get out of here!" yelled the other boy.

Alicia turned around to walk back into the building and took her book bag off her shoulder. She opened it and grabbed her English book. Before any of the three men realized it, she ran up behind the older man and shoved the hard-covered book into the base of the man's skull. The man let out a small scream and fell to the ground.

"Hey!" yelled the other boy as he reached out to grab Alicia's arm. Before he could take hold, Alicia kicked him in the testicles. By this time, Julian had caught his breath. As both the men lay moaning on the ground in pain, Julian grabbed Alicia by the arm.

"Come on! Let's get out of here!" Julian said as he pulled Alicia into the building. The two students walked quickly down the hall, past the principal's office, and exited the main entrance.

"I can't just leave. I have classes," protested Alicia.

"You're not the only one," replied Julian. "But it's either hanging around here waiting for those dudes to find us or calling it a day."

After exiting the building, they walked down the street to the bus stop. As soon as the first bus arrived, Alicia and Julian boarded. She moved to one side of the bus while he went to the back. As soon as the bus was far enough from the school, Alicia rang the bell to get off. Julian looked out the bus window as Alicia walked away, curious about the girl who had saved him. Although he was happy, Alicia had intervened, and the aggressiveness of the short, quiet girl surprised him. She was not at all as she appeared to be. Alicia had seemed so helpless when the girl stood trapped in the convenience store earlier that morning. He would've never guessed she could easily disable two men twice her size.

Finally, Julian got off the bus at the main terminal. After transferring to another bus, he rode the bus for another 30 minutes before finally arriving at the bus stop outside his apartment complex. Exiting the bus and walking towards his uncle's apartment, he saw his uncle leaning into a car in the parking lot.

"Hey, boy. Where are you coming from?"

"School."

"What, you have football practice or something?"

Julian nodded and continued walking.

"Hey, Julian. Let me holla at you," said his uncle as he followed Julian to the front door. Julian took a deep breath and sighed loudly.

"What is it, Uncle Dexter?"

"Hey, I need you to let me hold a few dollars until next week."

"How much?"

"Ten...I mean, twenty dollars."

"What? The money you took out of my bedroom wasn't enough?"

"Money out of your room? I don't know what you're talking about."

Julian shook his head. His money was gone forever, and he couldn't get it back. He reached into his pocket and pulled out a $10-dollar-bill.

"This is all I have."

"Ten dollars? That's it?"

"Most of my Money went to mom. You know that. This cash is all the money I have. Take it or leave it."

Dexter snatched the money from Julian's hand and returned to the car. Frustrated with his ungrateful uncle, Julian went into the apartment and slammed the door.

13

Daddy Time

After dinner, Alicia went to the living room to watch television with her father. For most of the day, her father was alone to fend for himself, and she felt terrible about that. But truthfully, although Alicia roamed the school hallways, the teenager felt alone, too. Her life felt empty, like a chalkboard wiped clean by accident, erased of relevance and all that she could've possibly been. She only felt at peace when she sat in the living room with her father. For that moment, the world melted away, and it was just Chuckles and her dad – as they had once been.

Alicia sat beside her dad on the sofa and turned on the TV. She quickly flipped through the channels until she found an old movie. She avoided the news because of the way it excited her father. Seeing a police officer sometimes sent him into a stuttering barrage of curses.

"Daddy, have you seen this movie before?" Alicia asked as she lay her head on his shoulder.

"No...no...I haven't," Alicia's father responded softly.

Alicia pressed her nose onto her father's shirt and breathed deeply. She loved the smell of his cologne. Although her father was injured, Alicia still found the little things that reminded him of who he was. He was a proud man before the assault, and although she had to help him onto the toilet, she did what she could to help him keep his dignity.

"Daddy, do you remember Mom?" she asked as they watched television.

"Yes...I remember your mom,' he replied, patting her head.

"Do you think about her sometimes?"

"Not a lot. She has...her life."

"Yes. That's true."

Alicia grabbed her father's arm. Life was so unfair to him. It wasn't right that her mother left a little girl to be raised by her father.

"And you, Chuckles? Do you have a boyfriend?"

The question surprised Alicia and made her stumble for a response.

"Me? No, Daddy. No boyfriend."

"It's okay...to...have one. You're a...pretty girl."

Alicia blushed and stood up.

"I'm going to get some water. Do you want something to drink, Daddy?"

"No."

As soon as Alicia reached the kitchen, the telephone rang.

"Hello?"

"Where were you today?"

Alicia sighed in frustration. It was Natalie's voice.

"I was at school."

"Four teachers reported you as absent."

"What are you, my prison warden or something?"

"No. I'm the next best thing. I'm your guardian."

"Look. I was feeling sick, so I came home early, okay?"

"Alicia, I don't need to remind you how important summer school is for you, do I? You already know the consequences of not finishing. Do you want to repeat grades?"

"Of course not."

"Then show up and do the work."

"Got it. Is that all?"

"Tomorrow, I'll be showing up at the school to pick you up after the last class. I'll see you out front."

"Why is that necessary?"

"Part of it is because you don't know how to follow instructions. But the other part is because we have an errand to run before I take you home."

"What errand?"

"Just be in front of the school when school ends."

Alicia hung up the phone and poured herself a glass of water. After drinking it, she returned to the living room to finish watching the movie with her father. Sitting on the sofa beside him, she saw him nodding off to sleep.

"Daddy?" she asked as she tapped her father on his shoulder. "Let's get you to bed."

"What? I want to see the movie."

"We can watch it tomorrow, Daddy."

Alicia moved the wheelchair close to the sofa and grabbed her father around the waist. As she lifted him from the couch, he whispered in her ear.

"My Chuckles."

After Alicia sat him down in the wheelchair, she kissed him.

"Always, Daddy. Always.

14 |

A Proper Introduction

Alicia had just placed her books in her locker when she felt a tap on her shoulder.

"Hey," whispered a deep voice. Alicia turned around to see Julian standing in front of her. She hadn't realized how tall he was. Staring up at him felt like she was looking up into the dark leaves of a tall tree.

"Hello," she replied as she looked into his brown eyes.

"You ate lunch yet?"

"No, not yet."

"Let's go."

"Okay."

Alicia followed Julian down the hallway and the stairs until they reached the cafeteria.

"You want to find us a table in the back while I go up and get us some lunch?"

"Sure."

"Pizza okay for you?"

"Yes."

Alicia walked to the rear of the lunchroom and sat at the empty table in the furthest corner. She hated being there. Sitting in the cafeteria grossed her out so much. There was not a clean table anywhere. There were rows and rows of people she didn't know, all stuffing their faces with cheap food while pretending to be happy. To Alicia, eating in the cafeteria was horrible. She'd only eaten there once since she came to the school, and after that one experience, she vowed never to return. She fancied that the servers filling the students' trays with disgusting food must be witches. How else could they convince so many children to ignore the slop they served daily? The strange low-budget aromas that invaded her nostrils made her want to run away more than it induced a desire to eat. But it wasn't just the disgusting food that repelled her. The place seemed to touch every nerve that annoyed her. The place was loud like all of the school's annoying sounds were there.

Moments later, Julian walked over to the table carrying two plates of food.

"Are you hungry?" he asked as he slid a pizza tray before Alicia.

"Not really," she replied. She didn't know how to tell Julian how disgusted she was with the place. Politely, she lifted the pizza from her tray and took a small bite.

"Thanks for helping me with that problem yesterday."

"I think we helped each other."

Julian smiled and took a bite of his pizza.

"Where did you learn to fight like that?"

"I don't know. I think I know how to protect myself."

"Protect yourself? Those guys would say that what you did was more than protecting yourself."

Alicia smiled, and Julian smiled back at her.

"Why were they here? That one guy looked old enough to be someone's dad."

"My ex-girlfriend. We broke up, and her family didn't like how I did it."

"Really? How did you do it?"

"I just stopped talking to her."

Alicia didn't believe him. In her opinion, women usually sent men to harm other men if they were an abusive jerk or a man who couldn't take no for an answer.

"Is that your final answer?" she asked.

"What do you mean?"

"I mean, I'm not a fool. If you don't want to tell me the truth, say so."

Julian took a big bite of his slice of pizza and wiped his mouth.

"I'll tell you what. Tell me why you were shoplifting, and I'll tell you why those guys were after me."

Alicia pushed her tray aside and gulped milk.

"No biggie. I took those things because I wanted to. It's not the first time I stole something, and it won't be the last. I like stealing."

Julian's mouth fell open.

"Wow. I was expecting a denial or maybe a story about needing lunch. I wasn't expecting this."

"What? The truth? Why would I need to lie to you? You couldn't even stop those guys from kicking your ass. Why should I give a fuck about what you think?"

Once again, Julian's mouth fell open. He stared at Alicia for a second before responding.

"Do you always talk like this?"

"Like what?"

"Telling people how you feel."

"Mostly."

"Those guys came here to beat my ass because I started a rumor about my ex-girlfriend. She started one about me, so I returned the favor."

"That must've been one hell of a rumor."

"It was."

"So, you're good at lying?"

"What?"

"I steal, and you lie. That's about it, right?"

"No. I don't lie for fun. But I'll do it if I need to get myself out of a sticky situation."

"Or hurt someone to get revenge."

Julian was silent for a moment. He'd never met a person so disconnected from civility. Although it was refreshing, he couldn't deny that it pissed him off a bit.

"My lying also saved your ass yesterday. Let's not forget."

"I can't deny that. By the way, what did you say to the cashier?"

"I told her that I saw three guys stealing in the back of the store."

"How nice of you."

"Hey, it saved you, didn't it?"

Alicia smiled.

"Thanks."

"What time is it?" asked Julian as he searched the cafeteria walls, looking for a clock. Alicia stood up and grabbed both of their trays.

"Yeah, it's time to head back to class," she said as she dumped trays and placed them atop the trash can. Julian pulled on Alicia's shirt as the two students headed towards the stairwell.

"Hey. Maybe we should exchange numbers."

"For what?"

"To talk. Who knows when you may need my lying skills or when I may need your fighting skills?"

Alicia giggled and looked away. It was the first time a guy had ever asked her for her phone number. Quickly, she opened her book bag and took out a pen and a piece of paper. She wrote down her phone number, ripped it in half, and gave it to Julian. Julian held his hand for the pen, and Alicia placed it in his palm. As she pulled her hand away from his, she felt her face flush. She was surprised at how soft Julian's hands were. As he placed the paper on the wall to write, Alicia looked at him closer. His arms rippled with muscles. Although his jeans weren't that tight, she saw that he had an ass so tight that she could bounce a quarter off it. Soon, Alicia's hormones took over. She wondered what he looked like naked. Although she'd never been with anyone, her mind became engulfed in naughty teenage thoughts. When Julian turned around to give her the paper, she barely heard him.

"Here you go," he said. Alicia took the paper and tucked it in her backpack.

"See you later," she said.

"Yeah. See you," Julian replied. As Alicia walked away, she looked back over her shoulder. Julian walked further behind her, but Alicia could tell he was checking her out. As soon as she reached the bottom of the stairs, she took off running with a massive smile.

15

Riding With Nathalie

Alicia stood in front of the school waiting for Natalie to pick her up when the final bell rang. Soon, the students began pouring out and heading to the bus stop to go home.

"You're not catching the bus home?" asked Julian from behind. Alicia turned to see Julian descending the stairs.

"No. I have a ride."

"From who? Your mother?"

"No. My Guardian. She thinks she's my mother," joked Alicia. Julian smiled.

"Okay. Whatever that means."

Soon, a car pulled up to the front of the school and blew its horn.

"Now I get the joke. Your Guardian's a white lady," exclaimed Julian. Alicia laughed and touched him on the arm.

"Hey, I have to go."

"Okay. I'll try to call you later."

Alicia couldn't help smiling at the sound of those words.

"I'll be home."

As she opened the door to climb into the car, Natalie looked around for Julian. When she didn't find him, she climbed into the car and they drove away.

"Who was that? A boyfriend?"

"No. Just a guy trapped in summer school like I am."

Natalie cracked a smile.

"He's cute. Go for it."

"Is that your motherly advice or your attempt at gossipy intrusion?"

"Gossipy intrusion? Big words, no?"

Alicia smiled and decided to turn the tables back on Natalie.

"Tell me something. Why are you still single?"

"Why?"

"You can't use Daddy and me as an excuse for your nonexistent love life anymore."

"I guess I just haven't found someone good enough."

"What's good enough?"

"You know—someone to love and respect you. I'm a big girl, you know. Whoever loves me needs to see more than a fat girl."

"So, you're going to sit back and wait? You could die of old age waiting for that man to appear."

"Listen to the high school girl giving advice. Aren't you something?"

"All I know is if I were you, I'd be out and about. I wouldn't be sitting at home waiting for Mr. Right to arrive on my doorstep."

"Life's more complicated than that. When you become an adult, you'll see."

Alicia was learning a lot about Natalie. She'd only seen her as overly nosey with no right to be in her life. It was now apparent that she assigned intelligence based on age.

"Can I ask you a personal question?"

"Sure. Go ahead."

"Are you close to your family?"

"I'm about as close as anyone is, I suppose. My dad died last year, and now it's just my mom and me."

"Is that who you're protecting?"

"Protecting?"

"From my dad and me. Is that who you're trying to protect from lawsuits?"

"Alicia, what is this? Michael told you this?"

"I'm not dumb, Natalie. You may not realize it, but I have an actual brain."

"We're not talking about this now."

Alicia could feel the anger building up inside of her.

"Hey. Let's change the subject. How were your classes?"

"Just like all the others. Boring."

The two women made small talk as Natalie maneuvered the car through the city. They stopped at a grocery store to buy fruits and veg-etables. When Natalie wasn't looking, Alicia stole a candy bar and some granola bars. After they left the store, Natalie pointed the vehicle to-wards Alicia's home and cruised through the mostly empty streets. They made small talk, but it was mainly Natalie who talked while Alicia ig-nored her. Finally, Natalie pulled into the parking lot of Alicia's apart-ment.

"Do you need me to pick you up from school tomorrow?"

"No. I'm okay."

"Okay. If the school tells me everything is on the up and up, I'll give you some breathing room. Take these groceries. Tell your father I said hello."

Alicia climbed out of the car, grabbed the bag of groceries, and slammed the door. She wouldn't give her father the greeting. Natalie had confirmed what Alicia and her father had suspected – everything was a ploy to protect Natalie's family from being held accountable. As Natalie's car sped away into the night, Alicia threw the groceries on the ground and spit on them.

"Fucking bitch," she whispered. After a few seconds, she took a deep breath of the night air and pulled her hair back. Alicia had to shake off the anger and frustration. There was too much to do before Julian called her.

16

Two Months Later

Alicia only had enough time to slide the casserole into the oven and shower before Julian arrived. Most of her day, she cleaned the house and ensured her father was ready for visitors. Now, she only had one hour left before her new boyfriend would arrive. Her nerves were over the top. Alicia flew around the kitchen like a rocket, wiping here and there and washing dirty dishes. Finally, after seeing how much time had expired, she headed to the bathroom.

"Daddy, I'm going to take a shower, okay?" she said as she wheeled her father into the living room to sit in front of the TV.

"Okay, Chuckles. What time is...he coming?"

"He should be here in an hour."

Alicia sprinted to the bathroom, stripped down, and jumped into the shower. As she lathered her face, she smiled beneath the bubbles. Who would've thought Alicia would be in a relationship? She certainly didn't. Alicia and Julian started by talking on the phone every day. It was nothing spectacular. They'd go through the customary greetings and cataloging of the previous 24 hours. They cracked the occasional corny joke and flirted with one another. But it wasn't long before the conversations changed. They each revealed small pieces about each other. She found out he was the quarterback on the high school football team. She admitted to him that she was an avid comic book collector. Soon, she was sitting by the telephone with a burning desire for it to ring. When he didn't call on his regular schedule, Alicia tried with all her might to suppress the need to ask Julian why he had waited so long to telephone her. Julian and Alicia seemed to grow closer with every call.

When Julian asked her to be his girlfriend, she thought he was joking. Although she'd never told him, Alicia thought Julian was handsome and considered herself out of his league. Alicia was cute but not the type of girl the guys in her school gawked at; her boobs were small, and she didn't wear tight dresses, highlighting her curves. Alicia's build was more of a tomboy than sexy. It was hard for her to believe that Julian could be interested in her. She intentionally downplayed who she was and highlighted all the things she didn't have compared to the other girls in school. But still, Julian persisted. Minutes later, when she realized he was serious about being her boyfriend, a warm feeling moved through her chest like hot caramel. It was a feeling she'd never felt before. Suddenly, her world changed. She no longer felt pedestrian. Someone could see her for once, and it was lovely.

Alicia agreed to be Julian's girlfriend on one condition - he needed to come to meet her father. She was so happy with the change in her life and wanted to share it with the person she loved most. Her father had endured so much pain; they both had. And although they both went through their days without complaining, the smiles on Alicia's father's face were fewer and fewer over the years. Alicia wanted to give him some joy. She could tell he was worried about her life. Underneath all the injuries, her father was still there. And just like any other father, she was sure that her father knew the burden his medical needs were having on Alicia.

Alicia dug through her closet after showering until she found her most attractive skirt, a red high waist pleated skirt she'd stolen from the local department store a few months earlier. It was the only skirt that didn't make her feel too fat and didn't show her butt too much. After putting it on, she twirled a few times in the mirror to ensure the look was okay.

"Perfect," she whispered. Alicia gave her hair the once over with her curling iron and applied some olive oil hairdressing to prevent her hair from frizzing. Just as she finished putting on her makeup, a knock came at the door. Alicia ran out of her bedroom and into the living room. She opened the door to see a nervous Julian holding a small white box in one hand and flowers in the other.

"Hi! Thanks for coming," said Alicia as she hugged Julian nervously.

"Hello," he responded as he stepped back to look at Alicia. "You look very nice."

"Thanks. You don't look bad yourself. What's in the box?"

"Just a pound cake I picked up from the store."

"How nice. Come in."

Alicia took Julian's hand and pulled him into the apartment. After placing the cake on the coffee table and taking the flowers, she introduced Julian to her father.

"Daddy, this is Julian. He's my boyfriend."

Alicia's father straightened up in the wheelchair as best he could and smiled.

"Hello...how are you?" he asked, extending his trembling hand to Julian. Alicia was a little nervous about the exchange. Although she had told Julian about her father's injuries, she hadn't told him about her father's tremors recently developed. Julian smiled and confidently took the man's hand in his.

"Hello, sir. It's nice to meet you." he said as he shook it firmly. Alicia beamed with satisfaction.

"Here, Julian. Have a seat here on the sofa. Can I get you something to drink?"

"No. I'm fine, thank you."

Alicia sat on the sofa next to Julian and took his hand in hers.

"Big..." mumbled her father.

"What's that, Daddy?"

"He's...big. Do you play...sports?"

"Yes, sir. I play football."

"What...position?"

"I'm at the quarterback position."

Alicia jumped into the conversation.

"Daddy, didn't you used to play football when you were younger?"

"Yes, Chuckles. I did."

Julian smiled.

"Really? What position did you play?"

"I...don't...remember..."

Alicia could see her father struggling with his memory and was about to jump in, but Julian continued the conversation as if he had never noticed the problem.

"Well, the position you played isn't as important as the fact that you played."

Alicia's father smiled at Julian's comments.

"Smart boy," said Alicia's dad. Alicia rubbed Julian's arm and stood up.

"Look, Daddy. I'm going to set the plates for dinner. Excuse me."

As she walked away from the two men, Alicia was elated. For the first time in her life, she truly felt happy. She could finally see the light in her father's eyes. For once, he wasn't just a sick man under the care of his young daughter. He was a proud father to a daughter. As she set the table, Alicia listened to the men talking in the living room. The conversation was primarily one-sided; Julian would ask a question, or her father would ask a question, and they both would try to find the answer. To Alicia, talking to her father sometimes felt like trying to breathe through a wet sweater. It was frustrating for her, and she avoided long conversations. But Julian didn't relent, and he quickly fought through each discussion. He moved to the next. And the next. And the next. By dinnertime, the two men were laughing like they were old friends. Alicia could tell that Julian had found a place in her father's mind that a daughter could never reach – male companionship.

"Okay, guys. Dinner's ready," said Alicia. She walked over and attempted to roll her father's wheelchair into the dining room.

"No...I can...do it," Alicia's father responded as he pushed her hands away. Alicia and Julian stepped aside and watched her father wheel himself into the dining room. Once there, he lifted himself out of the chair and sat at the table. Alicia's eyes filled with tears as she watched her father position himself at the table without assistance. After he was comfortably seated, Alicia and Julian took their seats at the table.

"Who wants to say grace?" asked Alicia.

"I'll do it," piped up Julian. He enthusiastically grabbed Alicia's and her father's hands and led the prayer. As the group closed their eyes, Alicia opened hers to stare at her boyfriend. She secretly thanked God for Julian's presence and prayed that he would always be in her life.

17

Stains

When Julian arrived at the apartment complex from dinner at Alicia's place, he noticed a lot of cars crowding the parking lot. As he approached the apartment, he could hear the thumping of loud music shaking the glass on the window.

"Shit," he mumbled as he twisted the doorknob to enter. His uncle hadn't told him that he was planning to have a party. If he had, he would've tried to find something else to do until the commotion was over. When he opened the door, Julian could barely see into the apartment. There were people everywhere. The air inside the condo was sweaty and filled with cigarette and marijuana smoke. In the corner of the living room was a middle-aged guy with large headphones spinning two turntables. Beside him were two large stereo speakers with lava lamps on top of them, blaring Frankie Beverly & Maze music.

Julian made his way through the crowd of people and into the kitchen. His uncle was standing in front of a large Styrofoam cooler.

"Julian! What's up?" his uncle yelled loudly. Julian could tell he was drunk.

"What is all of this stuff? What's going on?"

"I did it! I finally came into some money."

"Money?!"

"Thirty thousand dollars."

Julian looked around nervously at the people standing within earshot.

"Uncle Dex, maybe you shouldn't go around telling people..."

"What? That I hit the lottery? I don't give a fuck about people knowing that. Do you know why?"

Dexter leaned in close to Julian and whispered in a drunken breath.

"Because if anyone fucks with me, I'll blow their fucking head off with this."

He lifted his shirt to reveal a black handgun tucked inside of his jeans.

"What the fuck?!"

"That's right. It's one of the first things I bought when I got my money."

"What if you drop it? What if it goes off? Take that in your bedroom and put it away."

"I'm your fucking uncle. You're not mine. I know what I'm doing."

Julian backed away from his drunk uncle in frustration. No matter what happened, he wanted no part of it.

"I'm going to bed," he said as he pushed past his uncle. Julian walked to his bedroom and opened the door. As soon as he flipped on the lights, he regretted it – there were two drunken adults having sex on his bed.

"Hey!" he yelled. "Get the fuck out of here!"

He watched for a few seconds as the two people fumbled around, retrieving their clothing from various parts of the room. Disgusted by the fact that he'd have to clean up a stranger's sex stains before going to sleep in the same bed, Julian turned and stormed out of the room. He pushed past several couples dancing at the entrance until he was on the sidewalk. Julian stormed through the parking lot and down the street to the bus stop. He sat on the bench and stared into the darkness of the night. An uneasy feeling settled over him as he looked back toward the loud music. Something about what his uncle had said didn't sit right with him. The story seemed – off. He could tell his uncle wasn't telling the truth about his sudden influx of cash.

Julian lay down on the cold bench.

"Oh well. I guess I'll be here until that dumb fuck clears everyone out."

As the cars flew by on the road, he began thinking about his dinner with Alicia. He remembered how beautiful she was, the sound of her laughter, how she held his hand while he spoke to her father. Alicia was not Amisha. Unlike his previous girlfriend, something about Alicia made him want to be close to her. Sure, she was sexy. But it wasn't her physical beauty that moved him. There was something deep behind those big brown eyes. Julian could tell she had wisdom beyond her years. But he also sensed a deep sadness inside of her. There was sadness, fear, and - anger. Alicia seemed like a hunted animal looking into a hunter's rifle barrel, afraid of the gunshot yet wanting to attack the hunter despite the danger. Something made him want to know more about who she was. He wanted to be closer to her. To him, Alicia's spirit was like a warm campfire that was beautiful and dangerous all at once. The longer he held his hand above the flame, the closer he wanted his hand to be, knowing very well that getting too close could hurt.

18

The Irresponsible

Julian sat up suddenly and looked around. He hadn't realized it, but he'd been asleep for hours. He rose from the bench and looked over at the apartment parking lot. It was mostly empty. Grateful everyone was gone, Julian walked back to the apartment.

He almost fell when he entered the apartment; empty cans and bottles were all over the floor. The stereo speakers and turntables that had once been in the corner were gone. Sitting on the sofa amid all the clutter was his uncle. He was passed out and snoring, with a long line of drool stretching from his mouth down the front of his shirt.

"Uncle Dex! Uncle Dex!" Julian yelled. He walked over and shook his arm. His uncle mumbled, squinted at Julian, and then let his head fall back against the couch.

"I'm not cleaning this shit up." said Julian. He surveyed the messy living room table as he turned to go to his room. Suddenly, he froze. Sitting on the table beneath a few beer cans was the black handgun that his uncle had shown him earlier.

"Stupid motherfucker," whispered Julian as he carefully lifted the weapon from the table. He quickly walked to the backdoor and went outside. A white cinderblock sat on the edge of the backyard behind a large bush. After carefully placing the gun inside, he searched the backyard until he found another small rock. He put it on the cinderblock to shade the weapon from curious eyes. Julian went back inside the apartment and into his bedroom. After flipping his mattress over and changing his bedsheets, he fell asleep.

19

Summer's End

The final day of Summer School ended early. The students left class at noon, and everyone could go home. Julian waited outside of Alicia's classroom until the final bell rang. As soon as she came out, he kissed her cheek.

"Hey!" said Julian as she took her backpack off her shoulder.

"Hi, Cutie!" replied Alicia. She quickly pecked him on the cheek before any teachers could see her.

"What will you do with all the extra time?"

"I don't know. What did you have in mind?"

"The hospital is sending a medical carrier to take my dad for his annual check-up. We could relax at my house if you want. Maybe watch some TV?"

"You sure your dad's cool with that? I don't want to be in his house if I don't have his approval."

"Daddy's okay with it. It's not like we'll be doing anything. Just watching TV."

"Cool. You have snacks?"

"A ton."

"Okay. Let's go."

The Next Level

Alicia leaned against Julian's muscular chest and laughed out loud. Although the movie was a rerun she'd seen numerous times, Alicia still laughed at her favorite parts. Julian laughed too. It felt good to cut loose from school and relax a bit. Although he didn't enjoy the movie as much as his girlfriend, he enjoyed how her bare feet rubbed against his socks while watching television on the couch. Occasionally, Julian would put his lips on the edge of her ear and apply gentle kisses. He could feel Alicia's body tremble in delight every time he did so, and he loved it. Sometimes, she'd turn around to face him and look into his eyes. After delivering a deep kiss, she returned to her original position to continue watching the movie.

When the movie ended, Alicia stood up and looked out the window.

"Another hour, and Dad will be here," she said as she closed the curtains. Julian sat up and put on his sneakers. He didn't want to be in the house when her father came home.

"I guess I'd better go. I don't want to piss your dad off."

Alicia walked over to the television and turned it off.

"Wait. I want to show you something," Alicia said as she walked to her room. "Follow me."

Julian stood and followed her into her room. When he entered Alicia's bedroom, he smiled. Aside from the pink comforter and pillows, nothing was "girlie" about the bedroom. On several walls, there were posters of superheroes and comic books. Lined up on the wall beside her bed were boxes of unopened shoes, hair ribbons, and clothing with tags still attached.

"Wow. When you said you liked to steal, you weren't lying," exclaimed Julian as he looked around in astonishment. Alicia laughed at his words.

"Have a seat. I have something I want to give you."

Julian sat down on the bed while Alicia opened her closet. He laughed as he watched Alicia jump to look on the top shelf of the closet.

"Need some help?"

"No. I've got it."

After a couple more jumps, Alicia frowned.

"It's not here. Oh, yeah. I remember where I put it. Wait one minute. I'll be right back."

After Alicia ran out of the room and down the hall, Julian continued inspecting her bedroom. On her nightstand was a picture of a younger Alicia standing next to a man with a giant afro. Julian picked up the photo and looked closer at it. The man was Alicia's father. Julian smiled. Alicia's father looked like a hippy in the picture. He wondered if he liked smoking marijuana as his uncle did. He tried to imagine Alicia's father lighting a joint and smiled again. He never heard Alicia enter the bedroom.

"Hey," said Alicia. Julian turned around to see her standing in the doorway. She was completely nude.

Julian took in a deep breath and exhaled. His girlfriend's beauty was beyond anything he could've imagined. Alicia had unbraided her hair and let it fall around her shoulders. He could tell she had rubbed her body from head to toe in baby oil; her dark skin seemed to shimmer in the evening sun.

Alicia slowly crossed the room to stand in front of him. She didn't say a word, nor did she need to. Her chocolate eyes communicated her desire to be touched, to be pleasured, to be more than a frail girl trapped in a prison of anger and loneliness. Julian's knees weakened, and he sat on the bed before her. He was smothered in her beauty, her innocence.

As he stared into her eyes, it became apparent that she had planned this moment for quite a while. He could see her mind racing forward before he reached up to touch her face; her imagination had played out how she would give herself to the moment dozens of times.

As she leaned over to kiss him, Julian became nervous and afraid. The humiliation he'd endured with his ex-girlfriend was still fresh and annoying to him – like a mosquito bite. He started developing feelings for Alicia, but he wasn't sure if he was ready to reveal his deepest pains to her. Although Alicia was sure about giving herself to him, Julian was anything but confident. He was terrified. Julian didn't want to do to Alicia what he had done to Amisha. Although young, he knew real love was hard to find. If Julian and Alicia stood a chance, they had to be honest about their feelings.

Julian had to put a stop to their activities.

"Hey...hey..." he said as he grabbed Alicia's shoulders.

"What is it?" she whispered. Julian pulled her naked body close to him and laid her on the bed.

"We have to stop."

"Why? You don't have a condom?"

"No. It's not that."

"What is it?"

"I just think we're moving too fast right now."

Alicia's face hardened.

"It's another girl?"

"No. It's nothing like that."

"Then, what do you mean?"

"I just feel uncomfortable right now."

Julian grabbed the blanket on the bed and pulled the blanket between his body and Alicia's.

"Look. There are some things we need to discuss. I need to tell you some things about me. About my past."

"Well...talk. We have time."

"Not now. Your dad is coming home soon. Can we talk another day?"

Alicia pulled the blanket up to her chin.

"When?"

"I'm not sure. My schedule's a little busy this weekend."

Alicia looked away.

"Look. If you want to break up, say it. I don't have time for these fucking games."

"Alicia, look at me."

Reluctantly, she turned to look at him.

"I don't want to break up. It's not that. I think it's only fair if you know me completely before we move to the next level."

Suddenly, Alicia stood and left the room. As Julian sat alone in the bedroom, he wondered if he'd done the right thing. Julian liked Alicia and didn't want to make the same mistake of not explaining. Alicia had so much going on in her life, and he didn't want to be the one to make it more difficult. She didn't deserve that.

Moments later, Alicia returned to the room fully dressed. After pulling her hair back in a ponytail, Julian stood to embrace her, but she walked past him and started spreading the blanket neatly on the bed.

"My dad will be here soon. You should probably go now."

Julian knew she was upset and thought it wise not to press the issue.

"Okay. I'll call you later."

"Sure."

As Julian walked out of the apartment and closed the door behind him, Alicia grabbed the lamp on her nightstand and threw it against the wall, shattering it into a million pieces.

"Chicken shit, pussy!" she screamed into the empty house. Angrily, she threw herself onto the bed and burst into tears. She was humiliated by Julian's rejection, tormented by the reason he gave. Was she ugly? Unattractive? Maybe he was only humoring her by pretending to be something that she wanted him to be. Did he secretly have another girl in mind? Alicia's mind was all over the place.

After a while, a dull, thumping noise came into Alicia's focus. She looked at the clock on her nightstand.

"Daddy! Shit! I forgot!" she exclaimed as she jumped up from the bed.

Alicia rushed out of the bedroom. The glass from the broken lamp crunched on the bottom of her sneakers, and she almost fell. After regaining her balance, she made it to the front door and opened it.

"There you are. I thought no one was home, and we'd have to take your father back to the hospital," said the overweight hospital attendant as he stood behind Alicia's father's wheelchair.

"Hey, Daddy. How are you?" asked Alicia after kissing her father.

"Chuckles. I'm okay, baby. What's for... dinner?" he responded. Alicia smiled and pulled her father's wheelchair into the house.

"I'll order some Chinese today, Daddy. Is that okay?"

"Chinese...okay."

Alicia turned to the hospital attendant.

"Anything new?"

"Mr. Kelly has lost a little vision in his left eye. But beyond that, there's nothing to worry about."

The attendant leaned over to speak to Alicia's father.

"Mr. Kelly, I'll see you in a few months, okay?"

"Okay...see you...later."

Alicia closed the door and pushed her father over to the television.

"Do you need to use the bathroom, Daddy?"

"No, I...don't."

After turning on the television, Alicia grabbed a carryout flier from the kitchen and ordered Chinese food. When it arrived, she fed her father, washed the dishes, and went to her bedroom without eating. Her appetite was gone, and all she wanted to do was stay in her room and cry.

21

Winds of the Past

It had been a few days since Julian left Alicia's house, and the two hadn't spoken. He'd attempted to call her, but the phone was always busy. Sensing Alicia was probably taking the phone off the hook, Julian decided to camp out at the one class he knew she had.

Julian waited outside Alicia's class until the final bell sounded. As the students poured out of the classroom, he searched each face, looking for his girlfriend. Unable to find her, he touched one of the girls on the shoulder.

"Hey. Was Alicia in class today?"

"Yeah, but she left early. She wasn't feeling well."

Julian's heart sank. He missed Alicia and wanted to see her. Fearing that he'd made a mistake in rejecting her, Julian decided to go home and give her a call. He needed to tell her the truth about his past and wouldn't delay it further. Julian looked at his watch. He was supposed to be at football practice in an hour, but the thought of his mistake with Alicia was too powerful.

"Coach would never understand," Julian whispered as he walked through the halls. Love would never be a good enough excuse to override the Xs and O's of the gridiron, not with an old-school smashmouth football coach like Coach Jeffries. Julian began running through reasons he could give his coach for being absent. After racking his brain for a few seconds, he decided on the most generic excuse: he could always explain to Coach Jeffries that he had a family emergency.

"Yeah, that's it," he whispered. It was a generic excuse through and through because in a sense – it was mostly right. Losing Alicia would be devastating. Sure, Coach would make him pay for the missed practice on the field by having him run more drills, but the penalty for not speaking to Alicia was far more significant. He quickly ran out of the school building and to the bus stop, where numerous other students waited. He promptly boarded the first bus that pulled up.

As the bus drove off down the road, Julian softly banged his head continuously against the window.

"Am I in love?" he whispered to himself.

Internally, he answered the question almost as quickly as it came into his head. Yes. He loved Alicia. At that moment, he knew that he had fallen for her. Somewhere between the moment they'd shared their first kiss and the time he'd eaten dinner with Alicia and her father, he'd fallen in love with her. How she looked at him warmed his soul in ways no other person had. As he watched the passing trees, Julian began to feel anxious. He had to hurry home so that he could call her. Soon, he felt a fear that he hadn't felt before. What if Alicia gave up on their relationship? What if Julian never found another person? The regret of leaving Alicia's house without explaining his past to her grew more significant in his mind. Alicia had been willing to share it all with him - everything. Instead of being a man and explaining the situation to her, Julian's tongue had gotten stuck like someone poured glue into his mouth. It wasn't long before his fear became a full-blown panic.

Suddenly, the bus slowed down. The students sitting on the bus's left side stood and peered out of the window on the right side. Julian looked out of the window to see what was happening. Five cop cars were blocking the traffic up ahead. Several police officers were directing traffic while two others stood with their weapons drawn – aimed at two Black men lying on the street.

As the bus drove closer, the students pushed against the window to get a glance at the scene – Julian, too.

"Busted!" exclaimed a voice from the front of the bus. "I wonder what those guys got in trouble for?"

"Drugs, I bet," said another voice. Internally, Julian agreed. He knew four guys from his neighborhood who had gotten in trouble.

As the bus inched by the two men lying on the ground, one of the men raised his head to yell at the police officers. Julian's eyes widened. He recognized one of the men – it was his uncle!

22

Reconnect the Disconnect

Julian rushed into the apartment and dropped his books on the floor. He ran into his bedroom and picked up the phone without bothering to lock the door. He quickly dialed Alicia's number and held his breath. The phone rang twice.

"Come on. Answer!" Julian whispered. The phone rang twice more before someone answered.

"Hello?"

Julian collapsed on the bed.

"Baby," he said. Alicia paused before she responded.

"What is it?"

"I didn't see you in school today. Why didn't you wait for me?"

"I wasn't feeling well."

This time, it was Julian's turn to pause.

"Can we talk? Face to face?"

"Why?"

"I need to explain something to you. Can you come over?"

"Over where?"

"To my uncle's apartment."

"I don't think so. From what you told me, your uncle's place has always been full of people. It's a little too much for me."

"He's not here, and something's telling me he won't be around for quite a while."

"Why not?"

"I saw him getting arrested today."

Suddenly, Alicia's voice was urgent.

"Arrested? For what?"

"I don't know. But knowing my uncle, it's some bad stuff."

"Are you okay?"

"I'm fine. I passed my uncle in police custody while I was riding the bus home. The cops had him laid out on the street with handcuffs."

"Shit!"

"Can you come by?"

"I can't make it today because I have to care for my dad. Maybe tomorrow if we leave early."

"Deal. I'll cut out early."

There was silence on the phone for a few seconds, and then Julian spoke.

"Alicia?"

"Yes?"

"I love you."

After he spoke, Julian held his breath. He couldn't believe he'd told her how he felt.

"I love you too," Alicia responded. "I'll see you tomorrow. Okay?"

"Okay. Bye."

Julian hung up the phone, fell back onto his bed, and smiled. Saying the words to Alicia felt like a giant weight lifted off his chest. Now, he only had to prepare for how he would tell her about his past.

Suddenly, the telephone rang. Julian reached over and grabbed the phone.

"Hello?"

"Julian, it's me," said a raspy voice. Julian sat up. It was his uncle.

"Look. I got arrested. I need you to find me a lawyer."

"A lawyer? How am I supposed to do that? I don't have that kind of money."

"You have to figure out something. I don't have any other options."

"What happened to all that cash you had?"

"It's gone."

"Gone? How?"

"We can talk about that later."

Julian quickly ran through various scenarios in his mind. There were only two ways an idiot like his uncle could blow that kind of cash: gambling or drugs.

"What did you do?"

"Nothing."

"Don't lie to me. If you do, I'll leave your ass in there."

There was a slight pause before his uncle spoke again.

"They're saying it's drugs."

"They're saying?"

"Yeah, but I'm innocent. The dude I was riding with had coke in the car."

"How much?"

"I don't know. A lot...maybe."

"You fucking idiot! You used that money to buy drugs, didn't you?"

"Shhhh...not on the phone!"

"I'll search for a lawyer, but even Perry Mason won't be able to spring you if it's the serious weight. How much is bail?"

"I don't know yet."

"I'll do what I can, but I can't guarantee anything."

"Find an attorney. Don't let me rot in this place."

"I'll see what I can do."

"Okay. Thanks, Julian. Oh, and another thing."

"What? Finding an attorney to spring you isn't enough?"

"When you visit your mom, don't say shit."

"I'm not lying to my mom for you."

"She'll flip."

"You're her brother; she trusted you to care for her son. Now you're locked up because of drugs. She has every right to know."

"But if you tell her it could..."

Suddenly, the phone line went dead. Julian slammed the phone down on the receiver.

"Fucking dummy!" he yelled. "I hope you roast."

He wasn't going to help his uncle at all. He didn't want any part of his mistakes. He had his own life to sort out.

23

Revelations

Julian sat down on the sofa next to Alicia and took her hand.

"I missed you."

"I missed you too."

The two teenagers sat silently in the empty apartment, each waiting for the other to break the barrier that had separated them.

Suddenly, Alicia spoke.

"Your apartment is cozy," she said as she looked around.

"It's crap, but at least it's clean. I spent all day yesterday cleaning it up."

"Was it that dirty?"

"My uncle threw a party and never cleaned up."

Again, the two teenagers fell silent. Julian took a deep breath and turned to Alicia.

"Okay. I wanted to talk to you about what happened between us."

"You mean when you turned me down?"

"Yeah. It happened because I..."

"Julian, I'm a virgin."

Julian fell silent.

"Do you know how scary it is for a girl to give herself to someone for the first time? I was terrified. It took me days to get to that point."

"I know, baby. But let me explain."

Julian paused and lowered his head.

"Somebody molested me."

Alicia's mouth dropped open in surprise. She listened quietly as her boyfriend told her about his past. Julian explained how his next-door neighbor betrayed his mother's confidence and how his mother had murdered her for it.

While Julian spoke, Alicia didn't say anything. She moved closer to Julian and kissed his face as he poured out his past to her. Finally, he was silent.

"So that's the reason you wouldn't touch me. You were afraid. Now I understand."

Julian quickly turned to Alicia.

"No. That's not it."

Alicia looked confused. Julian took a deep breath and started pouring his heart out.

"The sex...the molesting...it did something to me."

"Of course, it did."

"No. You don't understand. It's like that experience became a part of who I am today. Now I find myself craving certain things about what happened to me."

"What do you mean?"

"I don't know. It's like I want the abuse. The name-calling. The physical domination. It excites me."

"Did you try to get help? Talk to someone?"

"That's the thing. I know I should get help with it. But the bigger part of me doesn't want to."

"You want to be this way forever?"

"It's just that I've accepted it as a part of me."

Alicia started crying, and she embraced Julian.

"I'm so sorry, baby. I didn't know."

"Remember that fight? I showed my ex-girlfriend who I was during sex. Once. But she didn't understand. She thought I was a freak of nature."

"So, you lied about her before she could reveal your secret."

"You're smart. Yeah, that's what happened."

Julian pushed Alicia away and moved to the recliner.

"Now that you know the truth, what do you want to do? Break up?"

Alicia thought for a moment before finally speaking.

"Was there blood or any wild stuff?"

Julian became angry.

"You see? I knew you wouldn't understand. Just go home, Alicia."

Julian stood and walked to the front door.

"Wait. I..."

"Maybe we can talk another day."

Julian opened the door and looked away from Alicia. As she walked to the door, she paused.

"Julian. Let's talk about this."

"No. You should go."

Reluctantly, Alicia walked past her boyfriend and was about to exit when suddenly, she stopped.

"No more running. I'm not leaving."

"Please, Alicia. Another day. I don't..."

Alicia grabbed the door and slammed it shut. Suddenly, she grabbed Julian by the throat and squeezed. Julian fell back against the wall.

"I said I'm not going anywhere," she growled. As she squeezed the fat of her boyfriend's neck, Alicia ran her wet tongue across his lips before kissing him. When she pulled back from the kiss, she looked into Julian's eyes. She was excited by what she saw: ecstasy and fear. The two emotions danced in his brown eyes like flames dancing in the wind. She could tell he wanted more. She grabbed him by the arm and led him to the sofa.

"Get on your knees," Alicia demanded. She smiled at the sound of her voice in the empty apartment. At that moment, she knew who she was: a powerful goddess utterly aware of what her boyfriend wanted and all she could do to transform the world around them into his tortuous playground.

Slowly, Julian lowered himself to the floor in front of Alicia.

"Alicia...I just..."

But Alicia instantly stopped him.

"Shut up!" she yelled.

"You speak when spoken to."

Alicia smiled as droplets of sweat appeared on Julian's forehead. He was panting when she gave him the following command.

"Remove your shirt."

Obediently, Julian peeled off his shirt. He sat trembling in excitement as Alicia walked around him. Without warning, she suddenly ran her fingernails deep into his back, causing Julian to wince in pleasure. Next, she grabbed a handful of his hair and yanked his head back roughly. Just as he was about to voice displeasure in the act, Alicia ran her tongue along his sweaty neck. Julian melted like hot chocolate in her grasp.

"Get up and go to the bedroom," Alicia instructed. Julian stood and instantly began walking to his bedroom. Suddenly, he paused.

"Are you coming?" he asked. Alicia walked quickly to him and once again grabbed his throat.

"Do what the fuck I say, do you hear me?"

Julian began shaking furiously and shook his head in agreement. After Alicia let go of his neck, she stood on her toes and kissed his neck down to his chest. Julian walked quickly to the bedroom. Alicia smiled. After waiting for a few seconds, she followed.

24 |

Melted Worlds

"What do you have planned two weeks from now?" asked Julian. "Nothing, as usual. Just homework and taking care of my Daddy," responded Alicia. "What did you have in mind?"

"I'll tell Mom to put us both on her visitor's list. You want to go?"

"You want me to meet your mom?"

"Yes. Unless you're afraid."

"No. I'm not. I'd love to."

Julian climbed out of bed. Alicia smiled as she watched his sweaty naked butt slide into his underwear.

"I'm going to grab a soda. You want one?"

"Sure."

As soon as Julian left the room, Alicia started laughing and kicking her feet hysterically underneath the blanket. She couldn't believe what the two of them had done.

"Holy Shit! I'm not a virgin anymore," she whispered. She'd heard stories from various people about how painful losing her virginity would be, but the experience for her wasn't all that bad. There had hardly been any pain at all. Sure, there was a little blood, but Julian had handled the moment like a gentleman and waited until she showered to change the sheets.

"I'm sorry, I don't have any ice," said Julian as he handed her a can of soda.

"That's alright," she replied.

Julian took a big gulp of his soda and placed the can on the night-stand. He leaned over and kissed Alicia on the lips.

"So…"

"So?"

"How was your first time?"

"Nice."

"I didn't hurt you, did I?"

"I'll live."

Suddenly, Alicia turned the tables.

"So? How was your first time?"

Julian blushed a bit.

"Nice. Although technically, it wasn't my first time. It was my second. But it was my first successful attempt."

"Did I do everything right?"

"To be honest with you, I don't know if there's such a thing as right and wrong."

"If you enjoyed it, then it was right."

Julian leaned over and kissed Alicia gently on the lips.

"I'm so in love with you. In time, we'll be able to…"

Alicia jumped in surprise.

"Oh, my God! What time is it?"

Julian looked at his watch.

"It's 6."

"Shit! I've got to go. Daddy hasn't eaten dinner."

Alicia leaped from the bed and started getting dressed. Afterward, she grabbed her purse and headed for the door.

"I'll call you when I'm home, okay?"

"Wow. No kiss?"

Alicia turned around and ran back into the room.

"I'm sorry, baby."

She wrapped her arms around Julian and gave him a deep-tongued kiss.

"Call me when you're home."

"I will."

As soon as she left, Julian sat on the bed and smiled. Life was changing for him.

What Daddy Wants

"Daddy, I'm home!"

Alicia walked into the apartment and rushed into the living room. Her father was sitting in his wheelchair in front of the TV.

"I'm sorry, Daddy. I was with Julian, and we lost track of time."

She walked over to her father and kissed him on the cheek.

"Chuckles. You're...home. How was your...day?"

"My day was good, Daddy. How was yours?"

"Kitchen..."

"I know, Daddy. You're hungry. Give me a few minutes, and I'll make us some dinner."

"Kitchen...Chuckles...kitchen."

"I know. I know. Give me a few minutes."

Alicia was starting to feel bad about spending time with Julian. Her dad was hungry and had been suffering while she was off exploring her sexuality. It wasn't fair for her father to be alone and hungry. She quickly walked to the kitchen and turned on the lights. When she did, she was shocked by what she found. There was food all over the floor.

"Daddy!" she yelled. "What happened?"

The kitchen looked like someone had released a miniature hurricane. There was uncooked spaghetti splayed out all over the floor. An empty carton of milk lay in the middle of the bed with black markings on it - the contents seemingly sprayed out as a wheelchair ran over it. The old margarine container that Alicia used to hold sugar was opened on the counter and laying on its side, most of its contents emptied onto the floor, and the cherry on top? A large pack of hamburger meat Alicia had recently stolen from the grocery store was open and brown in the middle of the mess.

"Maaaan...."

Alicia wanted to curse, but she couldn't. She loved her father and respected him. It wasn't his fault that he was injured. Angrily, she kicked the hamburger meat into the corner of the kitchen.

Suddenly, a grinding noise came from the refrigerator, which had been left open. Alicia rushed over and closed it. Alicia returned to the living room.

"Daddy, what happened to the kitchen?"

"I...was...trying to...spaghetti."

"But Daddy, you know you're not supposed to be trying to cook."

"Why...not?"

"Because that's my job."

"I can...take...care of my...self."

"I know, Daddy. But it would be best if you stayed out of the kitchen. Cooking is my job. Okay?"

"I know you...were out...with...Julian. I need to learn to take care of...myself."

"Daddy, no! Not in the kitchen."

"I'm a man! I can take care...of me!"

Alicia took her father's hand in hers and started to rub it. By his breathing, she could tell he was getting excited, and she didn't want to upset him.

"You're the man of the house, Daddy. I know. But the kitchen is mine. Please promise me you won't try to cook again."

"I can take...care...of myself!"

Alicia sighed in frustration. She wasn't getting anywhere with him.

"I know, Daddy. I know."

Alicia kissed her father's face and continued to rub his hand.

"I'll make dinner now. What do you want? Do you want baked fish?"

"Spaghetti, Chuckles. I want spaghetti."

"No spaghetti, Daddy. The meat is bad. Maybe tomorrow, okay?"

"Spaghetti..."

"How about some left-over chicken casserole? I think I saw that in the fridge. Hopefully, it kept. Would you like that?"

"Okay, Chuckles."

Alicia returned to the kitchen. After taking out the left-over casserole from the refrigerator, she sniffed it to be sure it was still edible.

"Thank God," she said as she placed the casserole dish into the oven. She turned it on and set her sights on cleaning up the mess. As she cleaned, she began thinking about her father. Although she hated cleaning up, she realized that the confusion was her father's way of trying to free her to live her life.

"Daddy, I love you so much," she whispered as she swept sugar into the dustpan. After cleaning up the kitchen, she went to the living room.

"Daddy, dinner will be ready in a little while. Okay? I'll tell Julian that I made it home okay."

Alicia picked up the phone and called Julian. He answered on the first ring.

"Hello, baby."

"Hi. I was starting to get worried. Is everything okay?"

"Yeah. Just making Daddy some dinner now."

"Good. Tell your father I said hello."

"Okay. I'll do that."

"What do you have going on tomorrow?"

"It's Saturday. Normally I would be going to visit Mom, but my dumbass Uncle needs me to find an attorney for him."

"Really? You want some company?"

"Sure, if you don't mind working a little."

"I don't."

"But after I finish that task, I have to go to football practice."

"Okay. I'll come home to make dinner for Daddy then."

"Cool. Okay, so I'll see you tomorrow at 10?"

"10 it is. Goodnight, love."

"Goodnight, Baby."

Alicia hung up the phone and went to her father's wheelchair.

"Julian says hello, Daddy."

"Oh. Is Julian coming for dinner?"

"No. Julian just wanted to be sure that I made it home okay."

"Nice boy. I like...him."

Alicia smiled.

"Yes, Daddy. I like him too."

26 |

What You Ask For

The sound of thunder startled Julian out of his sleep. Nervously, he sat up in bed, unsure of where he was. Large raindrops pounded against the window and seemed like they would crack the glass. Flashes of lightning made strange shadows appear on his bedroom walls.

Julian didn't want to admit it, but he missed his mother. He remembered their lives before the pain. When Julian was a little boy, Julian remembered how his mother comforted him. When the rainstorms pounded against his window, he recalled rising out of bed and feeling along the walls until he reached her bedroom. Once there, she'd throw back the blankets and allow him to lay beside her. She'd hum a song to him until the worst of the storm had passed. When the sun's rays peeked through the blinds, his mother was making pancakes and bacon in the kitchen.

"There's no need to be afraid of the rain," she'd say. "God is just doing his work."

Julian opened his curtains and looked out into the storm. It wasn't long before he was thinking of his girlfriend. He wasn't sure how things had progressed so quickly with her. His spirit seemed to feed off of hers. To the girls in school, she was terrifying. He'd walked with her through the halls and seen how most girls moved to avoid her. But to him, nothing was intimidating about her. He hungered for her aggressive behavior. Just the sound of her voice made him start to sweat. He thought back to how she touched, scratched, and criticized him. It was what he wanted.

But in his mind, Julian had another feeling pushing through. He was worried. What if Alicia's domination made him start to dislike her? Although there was a difference between what Julian experienced with Ms. Hicks and what he was now experiencing with Alicia, what would he do if his mind made the connection? What if the same thing happened with Alicia? Could he disconnect the negativity from their aggressive behavior without ending the relationship? There were no blueprints for him to follow. There was no one guiding him through this dark forest. For so many nights, he had longed for the touch of someone who would understand. Now that he'd found her, how would he know the limits of his pleasure without someone to tell him to pull back?

"Man. I'm sick as fuck," he whispered as he climbed back into bed. Suddenly, he picked up the phone. After pausing for a few seconds, he put it down.

"She's probably asleep, you dummy," he said.

He closed his eyes and let the sound of the storm wash over him. As the storm slowly moved away, he drifted off to sleep again.

27

Priorities and Consequences

The next day, Alicia went over to Julian's apartment. Although they planned to get an early start, things didn't go as planned. Instead of heading out to find an attorney for his uncle, they stayed in the apartment for hours, having sex. After their fourth round of making love, they took a shower together. When they came out, an idea struck Alicia as she was drying off.

"Hey. You may not need to run around the city to find an attorney. Use the phone book and call around."

Julian hugged her and kissed her on the lips.

"You're trying to keep me here, aren't you?" he said.

Alicia smiled and pushed him down on the bed. They again made love before Julian started calling attorneys from the phone book.

"My uncle's so fucking stupid," he told Alicia as he dialed. "Can you believe this dummy fell asleep and left a gun on the living room table?"

"He did?" asked Alicia. Julian held up his index finger as soon as the attorney's phone started to ring. He left a message with the attorney before hanging up and returning to his conversation with Alicia.

"Can you believe he did that? I had to take the weapon from him when he was passed out drunk."

"Did you give it back to him?"

"Hell no. I hid it in the backyard under a cinderblock. If I had let my uncle keep it, he'd probably be in prison for eternity."

Wisely, Alicia avoided the conversation. She realized that passing judgment on someone's family was usually a bad idea.

"I guess you're not going to football practice, huh?"

Julian looked at his watch and frowned.

"Coach is going to kill me. I've missed three practices this month."

"Well, I need to get home. The last time I was late, Daddy went into the kitchen and tried to make dinner for himself."

Alicia stood, kissed Julian goodbye, and headed for the door.

"Call me when you get home," yelled Julian as she headed out the door.

"I will, baby. I love you."

"I love you too."

28

Spaghetti

Alicia didn't go home right away. Instead, she stopped at the grocery store and purchased some ground beef. She was going to steal the food, but after her conversation with her boyfriend about his crazy uncle, she couldn't bring herself to do it.

When she finally reached her front door, the sun was beginning to set. Alicia unlocked the door and walked in. Her dad was sitting in a wheelchair in front of the television.

"Let's hope he didn't destroy the kitchen today," she whispered as she turned to lock the door.

"Hi, Daddy."

She went to the kitchen and put the groceries in the refrigerator.

"Daddy, I'm making your spaghetti tonight. That's what you want, right?" she yelled as she filled a pot with water. After removing the chopping board and washing it off, she took out a large knife, grabbed an onion, a green pepper, and cloves of garlic, and placed them all on the counter.

"Daddy, do you need to go to the bathroom?" she yelled as she walked back into the living room.

"I know you didn't go to the bathroom, Daddy. Let's get that taken care of before I start cooking."

As soon as Alicia was halfway to her father, she froze. Something wasn't right. His curled hand was an awkward fist resting on his lap.

"Daddy?"

Alicia started screaming as soon as she walked in front of her father. Her father's eyes were open, and as if looking through the television, the irises were milky, white, and glassy. His mouth clenched shut while bloody vomit dripped from his chin onto his shirt.

"Daddy! Daddy!"

Alicia grabbed him by both shoulders and shook him furiously. After she put two fingers on his throat to see if she could feel a pulse, Alicia screamed again. The coldness of his skin caused her to fall backward onto the floor.

"Okay, Daddy. You've just had a little accident. I'll call for help."

She quickly climbed to her feet and ran to the phone in her bedroom. She quickly dialed 911.

"Please. I need an ambulance sent to 151 Tuckerman Street, Apartment 1054. My father had a stroke or something. Please hurry."

The emergency operator continued to talk, but Alicia dropped the phone and ran back into the living room. She grabbed her father's wheelchair and pushed it in front of the sofa.

"Let's get you out of this wheelchair so you can stretch out."

Just as she had done before, Alicia slid her arms underneath her father's arms and attempted to lift him out of the wheelchair. As she pushed down with her legs, she grunted in frustration. She was unable to move him. Tears poured down Alicia's face, and her whole body felt weak. Attempting to lift her father felt like raising a giant piece of ice. She prepared to lift him for a second time but stopped and gagged. The familiar odor of urine and feces flooded her nostrils.

Alicia sat on the sofa before her father and grabbed his cold hand.

"It's going to be okay, Daddy. You just had a spell. The doctors will fix you," she cried. But her heart was gone, shredded into a thousand pieces. Panic was beginning to overwhelm her. As much as she wanted to believe the paramedics would revive him, she knew what death was. Her father was gone.

"Daddy, don't leave me," she cried. "I'm all alone."

She could hear the far-off wailing of sirens approaching, and she began negotiating with her dead father.

"Okay, Daddy. What if I show you how to cook? Will you come back? I promise I'll take care of you without complaining. I'll be your Chuckles, just like the old days."

Suddenly, she stood and threw her arms around her father's neck. The bloody vomit stained her shirt and felt like ice on her skin. But her emotions had moved her beyond restraint. She wanted her father. Even as the smell of death enveloped her, Alicia clung to her father. His body was a part of hers, and she didn't want to let go.

"Daddy. I'm making spaghetti tonight. Your favorite," she said as she climbed on his lap. She never heard the paramedics banging on the door. She put her hand over his eyes and closed them, ignoring everything around her. Finally, she opened her eyes again and kissed her father's cheek. After pressing her nose close to his neck to smell his cologne once more, she caressed his hair and embraced his lifeless body.

"Miss? Excuse me. Miss? Let us help him," a voice said from behind her. Alicia looked up to see a female paramedic standing beside her. Reluctantly, Alicia climbed off her dad and moved away as another male paramedic moved in. As she moved away from the group, two police officers appeared at the door.

"Has he expired?" asked one of the police officers to the paramedic.

"Yes," the male paramedic responded.

Suddenly, Alicia exploded.

"You killed him! You murdered my father! Get out! Get out!" she screamed.

Alicia lunged at the closest police officer and smacked his face. Surprised, the officer fell back into the doorway on his back.

"Grab her!" one of the paramedics yelled. But before the second officer could grab her, Alicia sat straddled atop the police officer, swinging fists at his face. Finally, the second police officer lifted the teenage girl off of his partner.

"You killed him! Fuck you! Fuck you!" she continued screaming.

The police officer slammed Alicia to the ground and pulled her arms behind her.

"Calm down!" he yelled, pulling his handcuffs from his belt. But Alicia was wild with emotion. She was screaming, growling, and laughing all at once.

"Hey, we're going to need you guys to sedate her!" yelled the officer as he struggled to get the cuffs on. The female paramedic ran over and pulled up Alicia's sleeve. A few seconds after the needle entered her arm, Alicia slowly relaxed.

"That's it. Calm down. Calm down," said the paramedic.

The paramedics brought in a gurney to remove Alicia's father's body. Minutes later, a second stretcher came to remove an unconscious Alicia.

When the World Leaves You

Alicia sat in the empty room, staring down at the floor. She hated hospitals. To her, the smell of the place was always disturbing. The scent of various cleansers floating through the air reassured visitors that everything was sterilized and clean. But Alicia knew the truth. The cleaners were there to hide the nauseating stench of death emanating from within the hospital walls. And now, somewhere within these walls was her father. Dead.

Alicia looked up briefly to see an elderly white-haired doctor talking with Natalie, and then she lowered her head again. She didn't want to see her – not now. Natalie was partially responsible for the moment Alicia was drowning in. Sadness, anger, frustration, confusion; all the emotions were swirling around her head. Alicia swung her legs back and forth as she sat on the edge of the hospital bed and bit the inside of her lip. She tried her best to stop herself from going crazy, but the moving car she was in was still spinning out of control, making her dizzy and sleepy, unable to find the off switch.

"Daddy. Where are you?" she whispered over and over. She'd overheard the doctor tell Natalie that her father was taken downstairs and transported to a funeral home. Nobody had bothered asking his daughter what she wanted. Like thieves in the night, they took her father's remains away with no regard for the girl drowning in tears.

"Be sure to give her these sedatives for a few days. If she doesn't return to normal, you may need professional help. I think she's going to need to talk to someone regardless."

"Thank you, doctor."

Natalie walked over to Alicia and took her by the hand.

"Come on. Let's go."

Alicia pulled her hand away.

"No. I want to see Daddy."

"Alicia, that's not a good idea now. Why don't we wait until tomorrow?"

"No! I want to see my Daddy now!"

Natalie looked at the doctor, and he nodded back.

"You ladies can follow me."

Natalie and Alicia followed the doctor out of the room and into an elevator. After the doctor pressed the button, Alicia moved into the elevator's corner, away from the others. Natalie tried to touch her arm, but Alicia recoiled. She wanted nothing to do with the woman. Her mind remained focused on getting to her father. When the doors opened, she rushed out of the elevator, waiting for the doctor to lead. She followed him down a dark, winding corridor with a brightly lit room at the end.

"Daddy," she whispered as they got closer to the room. Both the doctor and Natalie heard her and quickly looked away. As soon as they arrived at the door, the doctor stopped.

"Please give us a few moments to prepare for viewing. I'll be out to get you shortly."

As soon as the doctor was gone, Natalie moved closer to Alicia.

"Be strong, Alicia. You can do this. I'm here for you."

But Alicia didn't hear anything she was saying. She was trembling in fear.

Seconds later, the door opened, and the doctor came out.

"Please come in."

Alicia took baby steps into the room and paused. The room had an odor she'd never smelled before. After building the courage, she walked past the doctor and into the room. Two rows of bodies underneath white sheets were in the center of the room. The doctor walked to the closest one and lifted the sheet to reveal Alicia's father's face. Alicia felt her knees buckle and would've fallen to the floor if not for the doctor catching her.

"Daddy...daddy...daddy..." she cried over and over. She touched his face gently and kissed his forehead. The sight of daughter and father was too much for Natalie, and she began sobbing loudly. The doctor walked away from the two women and stood by the door, staring at the floor.

Suddenly, Alicia wiped away her tears and stopped crying. As if someone inserted a giant metal rod into her body, she stood upright and looked back toward the doctor.

"How did he die?"

"An autopsy needs to be performed. But from what I can tell, it looks like your father might've died from a stroke or a blood clot."

"And both of those resulted from his injuries, right?"

"I would say yes."

The doctor's answer seemed to make Alicia's body more rigid than before. Her nostrils flared, and the muscles in her jaws flexed as she bit down.

"What will you do with my father?"

"We're transferring him to a funeral home. From there, you can make arrangements for his burial."

Natalie interrupted the two.

"Don't worry about that, Alicia. I'll make the funeral arrangements."

Alicia turned back to her father.

"No funeral. Just cremate the body and give the ashes to me."

Both the doctor and Natalie looked at one another in shock. The coldness of Alicia's words was surprising to them both.

"Maybe you want to take some time to think about it. What about your father's family?" asked the doctor.

"I'm his only family, and I say burn him. Just return the ashes to me."

Alicia walked out of the room into the dark hallway without looking back at her father or speaking another word.

30

You Know

Alicia sat on the sofa, staring through the television. Images were flashing, but she didn't see them. All she could think of was how her father's face had looked in the hospital: cold and lifeless, his body nothing but a shell, vacant of her father's warm spirit. The grotesque way that his hand remained twisted bothered her; the mangled appendage looked claw-like, turned in the same fashion it had been when he had tried to fight off the stroke.

Alicia sighed deeply. Her father was gone. That thing lying back at the hospital wasn't her daddy. She knew that. It was absent of the sweet cologne her father always wore. Instead, what lay back at the hospital was covered in the rank stench of death. It was a sick joke to Alicia's senses. Even as she sat in the living room, the odor continued to invade her sense of smell. It was as if the corpse was lying in front of her.

"I know you told me that you're not hungry, but I'm making lasagna," yelled Natalie from the kitchen. "And for dessert, I baked a nice pound cake yesterday. I know you told me you're not hungry, but you've got to try to force something down."

"Okay," Alicia responded. Natalie walked to the living room and sat next to Alicia on the sofa.

"I know you didn't want to come to my apartment, but in light of everything that's happened, I didn't think it was wise to leave you alone in that apartment. Besides, you've never visited my place. How do you like it?"

Robotically, Alicia looked around the place.

"It's nice."

"Yeah. I don't like it so much. I'm thinking about moving next year."

Suddenly, Natalie jumped up.

"Oh! I'd better get dinner started."

After Natalie walked away, Alicia turned back to face the TV. Natalie's voice was an annoyance in her head, like a million alarm clocks ringing at once. Who cared about her apartment at a time like this? The comment was so out of place that it made Alicia grind her teeth to stop it from exploding. She wondered if Natalie realized how much she hated her.

31

Transformation

Alicia woke up to the sound of an infomercial playing on the TV. She grabbed the remote control sitting next to her and turned it off. After the TV's light died, Alicia noticed a small digital clock sitting on the table in the room's corner.

"4 am? Shit," she whispered as she stood and stretched. She flopped back down on the sofa, closed her eyes, and attempted to go back to sleep. Suddenly, her eyes popped open again. As she stared into the darkness, an enormous wave of anger overcame her. She began breathing heavily as her eyes darted from one side of the room to the next.

"They took you from me," she whispered. "Daddy! Daddy! Daddy!"

She stood up and was about to walk into the kitchen when she saw the poundcake on the dining room table – a large knife next to the plastic container.

"Her food. Bitch! Devil! Murderer!" she whispered. Alicia took the top off the cake dish and grabbed the knife. Slowly, she pushed the sharp butcher's knife into the cake until she felt the thud of the blade strike the table.

"If not for you, Daddy would be here..."

Suddenly, Alicia plunged the blade into the center of the cake again. She didn't understand why, but the feel of the knife penetrating the cake excited her. One satisfying thrust led to another. And another. Soon, the cake was nothing but a chunky pile of mess in the center of the table. Alicia looked at the cake and then looked at the knife. The anger boiling within her was out of control, causing her to sweat and take deep breaths. Suddenly, she looked at the blade in her hand. Without thinking, she opened her palm and ran the weapon across her palm, wincing in the darkness as the pain brought her back to reality for a moment. She couldn't see the blood coming from the cut on her hand, but she felt it; the oozing of the fluid from the wound crawled around her palm and dripped into the pile of cake on the table. She squeezed her hand open and closed, a frightening smile on her face as the sound of the sticky blood in her palm echoed throughout the room.

Alicia looked up at the ceiling.

"You," she whispered. Alicia walked out of the dining room with the bloody knife and started climbing the stairs. Although she couldn't see where she was going, she moved like a woman, aware of her surroundings. She slid her bloody hands along the white walls until she reached the top of the stairs.

"Where...are...you?" she whispered. The words were barely audible as they floated from her mouth. Softly, Alicia took step after step until she reached the bathroom. A few steps beyond the bathroom was a door with a dim light underneath it. Alicia stood in front of the door for a few seconds. Alicia could feel the storm gathering within her, preparing to unleash hell on Natalie. Her hands were shaking furiously. She grabbed the doorknob of the bedroom and twisted. She licked her dry lips, anticipating what she was about to do. Slowly, she pushed the door open.

As soon as Alicia opened the door, she saw Natalie sleeping in the center of a large bed; her eyes were covered with a floral sleeping mask, and she snored loudly. A melted candle sat on the nightstand beside her, flickering as her heavy frame pushed her breath throughout the room. Alicia gripped the handle of the knife and moved closer.

"You deserve this. You used us. You brought pain to our lives," she whispered as she moved closer.

Suddenly, Natalie started coughing. Alicia froze as she watched the fat woman cough uncontrollably in front of her. Alicia took one step back and was about to run out of the room when Natalie sat up and snatched the sleeping mask off her face. After reaching for the water glass next to the candle, she noticed Alicia standing in the room. Instantly, Alicia dropped her hand and hid the knife behind her back.

"Alicia?"

"I...just..."

"What is it? Is everything okay?"

Natalie could see that Alicia was holding something behind her back.

"What's that?"

"Oh...this?'

Alicia pulled out the knife.

"I was going to get a slice of cake, and I came up to see if you wanted to have a slice with me."

Natalie's face turned as white as a sheet.

"Uh... I'm exhausted. I..."

Alicia sensed that Natalie had figured out why she had visited the room.

"I just wanted to talk about Daddy."

Natalie started speaking fast.

"We can talk tomorrow if you want. Is that okay? I have a big appointment, and I need to get some sleep. Can we talk tomorrow?"

Alicia gave Natalie a weak smile.

"You know, it's okay. Maybe we can talk a little later. No problem. Go back to sleep."

Alicia turned and left the room. As soon as she was outside the room, she heard the door slam shut and lock behind her. Alicia chuckled under her breath and walked downstairs. After tossing the knife onto the sofa, she left the house and caught a bus home.

32

Do What You Say

Julian tossed and turned in his bed, trying to go to sleep. He was worried. Although it had only been a day since Alicia left his apartment, she had not called him to check in. They had spoken every day since they became a couple, and this was the first time in months they had missed a conversation.

Julian grabbed his phone and dialed Alicia's number. After it continuously rang without a response, he slammed the phone down on the receiver.

"Fuck!" he yelled.

He thought about all the possibilities for her absence. Was she angry with him? Had he said something stupid? Maybe her dad wasn't feeling well.

After thinking about all the possibilities for over an hour, his eyelids became heavy. Julian got on the phone once more and called Alicia. Still no answer. Frustrated, he drifted off to sleep.

33

Dreams Do Not Care

Julian looked around the room. There were children everywhere. They all wore birthday hats and were smiling as they ran back and forth through the room. An enormous chocolate cake was in the center of the table covered in candles. Julian stood to walk closer to the table, but something held him back.

"Not yet, baby," said a voice from behind him. "We have to sing Happy Birthday before we eat the cake."

Julian turned around to see his mother sitting on a sofa, holding his hand to prevent him from getting a slice of cake.

"Okay, mommy," Julian replied. A small boy and girl sprinted by him, holding hands, and crashed into the pile of balloons on the floor. After seeing how much fun the children had, Julian ran towards the bundle of balloons. One popped as he tumbled amongst the pile of balloons, causing the other children to scream in delight.

That's when Julian saw her.

On the other side of the room was Ms. Hicks. In one hand, she was carrying a belt; in the other, she had a plate of cookies. Julian ran to his mother's side and grabbed her skirt.

"No, mommy. I don't want to go."

Julian's mother smiled and patted his head.

"It's okay, baby. It's just for a little while. Mommy needs to go to work now."

"But...she..."

Ms. Hicks started walking across the room. The belt was gone, but she still held a plate of cookies. Julian turned to his mother again.

"Mommy. She's…"

But Julian's mother was gone. So were the children and balloons. The light in the room drained away. The only thing that remained in the center of the floor was an old black and white television with cartoons playing.

Julian turned to run out the door, but the door was gone. There was only a dark corner. Julian lowered himself to his knees and placed his head in the corner. He felt cold fingers on his neck. A demonic voice echoed throughout the room.

"If you don't, I'll tell your mother."

"But I don't want to."

"I'll tell…"

Julian turned around to see a ferocious rottweiler growling over a bowl of red mush. The beast scared Julian so much that he began screaming.

"If you don't eat it, I'll tell…"

"I don't want to. Please…" Julian begged.

"Eat it! Now!" the voice bellowed. Suddenly, the rottweiler leaped over the bowl and locked onto Julian's arm. He screamed out in pain as the monstrous animal clamped down on his arm. Without warning, the animal threw Julian to the other side of the room.

"AAAAAAHHHHH!"

Julian sat up in his bed, covered in sweat.

"Mom!" he yelled. But there was no answer. Julian looked around in the dark. After remembering where he was, he fell back onto his pillow and rubbed his face. Although tired, he didn't sleep for the rest of the night.

34 |

Through Darkness

It was six in the morning when Alicia arrived home from Natalie's house. Although the sun had just started to rise, she was exhausted. Slowly, she unlocked the front door and pushed it open. The lingering scent of her father's cologne was still in the air. She tried to ignore the haunting thoughts of her father and press into the apartment, but sadness washed over her. She was expecting to see her father sitting in his wheelchair, watching television. Instead, someone had pushed her father's empty wheelchair to the corner of the room.

Overcome with emotion, Alicia hurried through the apartment to her room. After sitting on her bed for a few seconds, she decided it best to shower. Although her father's death was still fresh in her mind, Alicia hoped to close her eyes and sleep for the whole day. She looked at the phone and considered calling Julian but decided against it. Everything was just so fresh in her mind, and Alicia didn't know if Julian could understand the mush that was her thoughts. She was just too tired to try.

"I'll call him when I wake up," she told herself as she climbed out of her clothes. She went into the bathroom and turned on the hot water. She stared at herself in the mirror and watched as the fog enveloped her. Soon, the steam from the shower fogged the mirror entirely, and Alicia watched her face disappear in the mist. When she could no longer see her face, she burst into tears. Alicia was so tired of life. Her life was so hard that she doubted she could stand much more. Now that her father was gone, the girl felt truly alone. Although she loved Julian, there was a great emptiness in the center of her. There was no connection to her childhood from which she could draw strength. From now on, all her emotional connections will be new creations based on her successes and failures. She was a tiny island, alone in the ocean.

Alicia finished showering and returned to her bedroom. Just as she dressed for bed and slid into the sheet, she heard a whisper.

I am here. You know it.

Startled, she looked around the room. There was no one.

"Maybe it's my imagination," she said. After all, it had been almost two days since she slept. Resigned to the possibility that fatigue was getting the best of her, Alicia climbed into bed and closed her eyes. Seconds later, she was sound asleep.

It was 10 pm when Alicia opened her eyes again. She climbed out of bed and went to pee. In the darkness, Alicia sat on the cold toilet seat and sighed. She somehow felt more depressed than she did when she initially went to sleep. Alicia felt the pangs of depression tugging at her soul. No matter how often she tried to pick herself up from life's hits, something always knocked her back down.

"If there is a God, he hates me," she whispered into the cold bathroom.

That is when she heard it again.

I know you hear me, don't you?

Alicia almost fell off the toilet bowl when she heard the whisper. She didn't bother wiping herself. She slammed the door shut and turned on the bathroom light.

"Who's there?" she asked loudly. She pressed her ear against the door to see if she could hear someone walking around outside. She couldn't hear anything.

"Who's out there?" she asked again.

But no one responded.

"I said, who's there?" she yelled again, pressing her shoulder against the locked bathroom door. Still, there was no response. Alicia was puzzled.

"Am I imagining things? Is it me?"

They murdered me!

Alicia screamed out in horror. The voice seemed to be coming from inside the bathroom. She frantically unlocked the door, slammed the door behind her, and ran out into the hallway.

She sprinted into the kitchen. After banging her foot into the trashcan and falling face-first onto the floor, she sprung to her feet. She felt around the countertop until, finally, she could grab a butcher knife from the knife block. She turned around and pointed the knife into the darkness.

"Whoever you are, I've got a knife, and I'm not afraid to use it," she yelled.

There was only the sound of the fall wind blowing through the trees outside the apartment.

Alicia peered around the kitchen wall into the dark hallway. She could see that the bathroom light was still on, but she didn't see movement underneath the door. Alicia inched down the hallway towards the bathroom, knife ready to slice at anything that moved. As she stepped gingerly past the door, she locked underneath. A shadow suddenly moved beneath the door, and Alicia dropped the knife. She took off, running down the hall and into the living room. She almost ran out of the front door when she froze.

"Aaaaah!" she screamed out in horror.

Sitting in a wheelchair in front of the TV was her father!

Alicia fell to her knees and began sobbing.

"Daddy...Daddy...Daddy..."

Slowly, Alicia's father turned to look at her; his milky white eyes opened wide and fixed on his daughter. Suddenly, his mouth jerked open; red vomit began pouring out.

"Chuckles. Help me," Alicia's father said as he gasped and choked on the vomit. He raised his hand towards Alicia, beckoning for her to come closer.

"Come to me, Chuckles. Help me to the bathroom," he begged.

"You're not my daddy! He's dead!" Alicia sobbed.

Suddenly, her father's voice became demonic.

"I'm a man! I'm a man!" he growled. Alicia watched in horror as her father's hand twisted and contorted as he began to convulse violently. She covered her ears, trying to block out the sounds of the bones in her father's arm, the cracking, popping sounds the bone made as it twisted into the same grotesque position she'd found him in.

"It's only your imagination," she said. "When you open your eyes, Daddy won't be there." She closed her eyes and counted to ten. When she opened her eyes, her father was gone. She quickly grabbed the remote from the table and turned on the TV. After raising the volume as loud as she could, she dropped the remote on the floor. Slowly, she backed out of the living room and ran into her bedroom. Alicia locked the door, dove into her bed, and pulled the covers over her head.

"This is just your imagination. It's not real," Alicia said as her hot breath filled the blankets. "Daddy's gone."

Alicia squeezed her eyes shut, praying for the morning to come quickly. But time moved slowly. Beneath the blanket, she looked at her watch; only thirty minutes had passed since she started hiding. Soon, her curiosity started gnawing at her. It wasn't long before she doubted everything that took place.

"Did I see my dad? Who was in my bathroom? Were the whispers something I conjured in my head? Maybe I imagined the whole thing."

After a while, Alicia threw the covers off her head and looked at the bedroom door.

"This is ridiculous. Why am I afraid? I'm the only person here," she whispered. She could see the light shining beneath her bedroom door. Still afraid and slightly ashamed of herself, Alicia climbed out of bed and was about to turn on the bedroom light when she saw a shadow beneath her door. Her breath turned into a lump of ice in her throat. She tried to run but couldn't. Her whole body was a block of ice frozen in fear. Suddenly, a terrifying whisper rang out in the room.

What are you going to do about it?
Alicia moved away from the door.
"Who are you? What do you want?" she asked.
You know.
"I don't!"
You do! No rest until you finish the job!
"What job?"
You know...you know.
"Daddy? Is that you?"
You must do it!
"Daddy! Why did you leave me?"
Away. Awaaaaaay.
The fear melted away from Alicia, and she moved closer to the door. The shadow was still there, moving side to side.
"Will it be difficult? How do I start?"
You know. You know.
"With her? Is that who you mean?"
The whisper was silent.
"Natalie? Is that the person you want?"
Noooooo.
Alicia thought for a moment before speaking again.
"You want me to kill someone?"

Yeeeessss.

"Who? Tell me. Who do you want me to kill?"

Them. Them. Them.

Suddenly, a thought entered Alicia's mind. She stood and opened the door. No one was there.

Yes, yes.

"But how do I..."

Alicia stopped. As quickly as she asked the question, she had the answer.

Yes. Him.

Once again, Alicia smiled.

Behind the house. Under the block.

"When should I start?" asked Alicia. There was only silence.

"Tell me. When should I start?" Alicia asked again. There was still no response. Alicia closed her bedroom door and returned to her bed. After she settled underneath the blankets, she looked at her door again. The shadow was gone. Alicia reached over, grabbed her phone, and dialed Julian's number.

35

Different Kisses

"Hello?"
"It's me."
Julian was quiet for a moment before speaking.
"Why haven't you called?"
Alicia took a deep breath.
"Daddy. He died."
Julian sprang up out of his bed.
"What?!" he said as he stumbled to turn on the light. "How? What happened?"
"He had a stroke or something."
"Are you okay?"
"No. I'm not."
"Where are you?"
"I'm home."
"Baby. Are you serious? It would help if you weren't alone in that apartment. Not after something like this."
"I was at Natalie's house for one night, but things got too weird."
"Do you want me to come over?"
"No, I'll be okay."
"You shouldn't be alone right now."
"Can I come over to your place?"
"Absolutely. Do you want me to come and get you?"
"Just meet me at the bus stop in front of your apartment."
"Okay. How long?"

"An hour?"

"Okay. See you then."

Julian hugged Alicia as soon as she got off the bus. He didn't realize how much he missed her.

"Hey. Let's get inside," Julian said as he wrapped his arms around her shoulders. As soon as the two lovers arrived inside the apartment, Alicia burst into tears.

"He's gone. Daddy's gone," she cried. "What am I going to do?"

Julian couldn't do anything but hold her close. He knew the feeling of loneliness too well. When his mother had gone to jail, he cried every day for six months.

"Come. Let's sit on the sofa. Let me get you something to drink."

Julian went to the kitchen to retrieve a glass of water. After pouring himself and Alicia a drink, he looked at the backdoor. With Alicia in the apartment, his uncle's sudden arrest made him uneasy. He was sure he owed people money, and in time, they could show up at the apartment to collect. He placed the two glasses on the counter and retrieved a chair from the dining room. After positioning the chair underneath the doorknob, he returned to his girlfriend.

"Here you go," he said as he passed the glass to her. Alicia took the glass of water and wiped the tears from her face.

"What am I going to do? Daddy was everything to me."

"What about your mom? You ever try reaching out to her?"

"No. I wouldn't even know where to begin."

Alicia took a sip of the water and sighed.

"It's just me, I guess."

Julian sat down his glass on the table. He pulled Alicia close and embraced her again.

"You aren't alone. You have me."

Alicia started crying again.

"Don't say it if you don't mean it."

"I do mean it. I'm yours. Completely."

Alicia raised her tear-filled eyes and stared at Julian.

"One day, you're going to leave me. I know it."

Julian's face hardened.

"I promise you. I won't. No matter what problems we have. If you love and respect me, I will never leave."

"Why? I'm a world full of problems."

"Because you took the time to love me when no one else would. You accepted me and all my issues. Why would I abandon you in your time of need?"

Alicia gave Julian a lengthy kiss.

"Words are always sweet, but you'll have to prove your love one day."

Julian smiled.

"How about we prove it next Saturday?"

Alicia looked startled.

"Next Saturday?"

"Remember I told you I'd put you on my mom's visitor list? She did it. You want to go?"

Alicia bit her lip.

"I don't know, baby. I don't know if I'll be in the visiting mood. I might be a little off."

"A change of scenery might be just the thing you need. Granted, it's a prison, but mom has always been the best with lifting spirits."

"I just don't…"

"Come on, baby. You asked me to prove how much I love you. I'm trying."

Alicia cracked a small smile.

"Okay. Let's do it. I'll go with you."

"Cool. In the meantime, you can stay here with me."

"Here with you?"

"Yeah. You shouldn't be staying in that house alone."

"But what about your job and football?"

"Well, Coach benched me for missing practices. I won't be playing for two games."

"Because of me? I'm sorry."

"No. It wasn't because of you. Mostly me, my dumb-ass uncle, and a few other things. But not you."

"You sure I won't be interfering?"

"No. Get enough clothes for one week, and we'll return to my place, okay?"

"Okay."

Alicia hugged Julian and closed her eyes. Moments later, the couple fell asleep.

36

It Would Be Best If You Were Not Here

Julian sat waiting in the living room while Alicia took a shower. As he looked around the room, he couldn't help feeling sad. Alicia's father had been so nice to him. He remembered the dinner they shared when he first met the man. Although injured, Julian placed his kindness at the head of the table. It was an honorable gesture. One that Julian would not soon forget. And now he was gone.

Soon, Julian's eyes fell on the wheelchair sitting in the corner of the room. He wondered how his girlfriend could cope with being in the apartment alone. The sight of the empty chair brought tears to his eyes. Feeling that his emotions were getting the best of him, Julian stood and walked down the hallway to Alicia's bedroom.

"Babe? You ready?" he yelled to the hallway. As he approached Alicia's bedroom, he heard her speaking.

"You on the phone?" he asked. Expecting to see his girlfriend on the phone, Julian pushed the door open and paused. Alicia was in her bra and panties, sitting on her bedroom floor with her back to the door. Instead of getting dressed, she was in a heated conversation – with no one.

"Is that what you want? Just tell me!" she said. "I miss you so much! But if you tell me, I have to…"

Alicia turned around suddenly and saw Julian standing in the doorway.

"What are you doing?" he asked, staring incredulously at her. Alicia climbed to her feet.

"Nothing. Just trying to talk with Dad."

"Trying?"

"I know he's gone, but sometimes it helps me to pretend he's here."

Julian moved closer.

"Are you sure that's it? Maybe you need some help."

Alicia pulled on her jeans.

"We all need help. You're not saying anything new."

"No, baby. I mean, professional help with your loss."

Alicia got angry.

"You mean like the help you need for your S&M fetish? Don't judge me!"

Julian shrank against the wall and lowered his eyes to the floor.

"I'm sorry, Alicia. I didn't mean..."

"Look. I'm trying my best to handle things, but I'm barely holding it together. I need you to be my lover. But more than anything, I need you to be my friend. Not my judge."

Julian felt bad. He realized that he should've kept his advice to himself. He went to Alicia and hugged her.

"I'm sorry, baby. Can you forgive me?"

"It's okay, love. Let's go. Being in this house brings up too many bad feelings."

Alicia finished dressing, and the two teenagers left the apartment.

The Plans

Alicia climbed out of bed and put on Julian's t-shirt. After ensuring her boyfriend was asleep, Alicia walked out of the bedroom and softly closed the door behind her. She tiptoed through the hallway and into the kitchen. She removed the chair from the back door and opened it.

When she left the apartment, Alicia took a deep breath. The stars danced in the night sky. Unlike the parking lot in front of the apartment, the backyard was quiet and peaceful. No noisy neighbors were present, only a tiny girl moving softly through the night. She smiled as the dew-covered grass brushed over her toes. The soft chirp of the crickets filled the night air. A few of them paused as Alicia moved through the grass and started up again once she had moved beyond their untraceable location.

Soon, Alicia stood in front of the trees at the yard's edge. It was hard to see into the bushes, so she walked back and forth, looking on the ground. Soon, her eyes fell on the block of concrete sitting behind a bush. She walked into the bushes and shoved her hand into the middle of the cinderblock. Instantly, her hand fell on the cold metal handle of the gun. She lifted it out and backed out of the bushes. After walking back into the moonlight in the backyard, she held the weapon up for inspection.

"I have it. Now, what do you want me to do?" Alicia asked.

After waiting patiently for a few seconds, she heard the voice respond.

Find them. Kill them.

"But how? I don't know who they are."

If not them, find others like them.

Alicia began to tremble in the darkness.

"But...they're innocent...with families. That's..."

Muuuurderrrr.

"I can't do that."

You will!

Alicia looked more closely at the weapon.

They took everything. You must!

"Maybe I could..."

There's no time for that! Kill!

Alicia wiped the mud from the gun handle with her shirt.

"I will! For you, Daddy..." she whispered as she aimed the gun at the bushes.

Yeeesss! Muuuurderrrr.

"I will kill them."

After tucking the gun into her t-shirt, Alicia went back into the apartment. Once inside, she put the weapon inside her bag of clothes, removed the t-shirt, and slid back into bed with Julian. She moved closer to her boyfriend and smiled. Tomorrow night, Alicia would get her revenge.

38

Waiting For Revenge

The next day was Sunday. Julian had to go to work, and the two agreed to meet at the shopping mall later that night. After he left for work, Alicia didn't know what to do. She spent most of the day sitting alone in the apartment, trying to think of anything other than what she was about to do later that night. Alicia tried watching a few movies to take her mind off it, but the focus was impossible. The forthcoming event made her anxious, so she cleaned Julian's bathroom, kitchen, and bedroom. By noon, she had done their laundry and dried it.

After making lunch, she decided to try to watch TV again. There was a movie that she used to watch with her father. As she watched it, her mind drifted back to when she was a child and all she and her father had lost on that fateful day. Although many years had passed since the police assaulted her father, Alicia still felt the oppressive heat of the car on that day. The awful sound of the nightstick on her father's skull crushing it and ultimately crippling him. The asshole smile on the police officer's face as he threw her father onto the street like he was a piece of trash.

Alicia got angry and turned off the TV.

"Tonight, I make you fuckers pay," she whispered.

After showering, Alicia threw on some jeans and was about to put on a blouse when she paused - a black hoodie was hanging in Julian's closet.

"Perfect," she exclaimed. After she put on the hoodie, she stood in the bathroom mirror to look at herself. The hoodie was much more oversized than her tiny frame, but she didn't care. She knew Julian probably would be surprised she was wearing his clothes. But Alicia needed stealth for what she had planned, and the hoodie was the only thing she could find. She grabbed the gun out of her bag and tucked it into the side of her jeans.

Alicia left the apartment and walked to the bus stop. She looked at the horizon as she sat waiting for the bus to arrive. The sun had almost completely disappeared. Brilliant rays of gold and orange made the trees appear on fire. Alicia felt an emotional connection to the sunset. For so many years, she had been a raging inferno inside. Now, the only thing that could cool her anger was revenge. And she would get it no matter the cost.

Her thoughts so consumed Alicia that she didn't hear the bus pull up. She instinctively boarded the bus but was unaware she'd done so. She felt the cold air passing through the slightly open window after the bus started moving. Her mind was like a shaken soda, bubbling with emotion and about to explode on the first person who opened it. There was no nervousness. No fear. Only anger squeezed through a pressurized chamber of intent. Alicia was a woman determined to commit murder.

39

The New Revenge

"Hey, baby," said Alicia as she walked behind Julian. He smiled and turned around, expecting to see Alicia. Instead, he saw a tiny girl in an oversized hoodie.

"Alicia?"

"Yeah, it's me."

"Why are you dressed like that?"

"I think I'm coming down with a cold or something. I didn't have a jacket, so I grabbed your hoodie from the closet. I hope you don't mind."

Julian took a step back and looked at her.

"You're dressed like a dude."

"Don't be a sexist jerk, baby. I wasn't feeling well."

Julian looked around to see if any of his coworkers could see them. After seeing a group of men exiting the restaurant, he pulled Alicia toward the bus stop.

"Let's go."

Julian sensed something was different as the two lovers walked to the bus stop.

"Is everything okay?"

"What do you mean?"

"You seem a little off tonight."

Alicia didn't respond.

"Did something happen today?"

"No."

"Okay."

As soon as the bus arrived, they got on and sat down in the bus's rear. Finally, Alicia spoke.

"Can we go get a coffee or something?"

"Coffee?"

"Yeah. I'm not feeling well, and coffee would help."

"Can't we stop at a grocery store and buy some to take back home? I'm a little tired from work."

At that moment, the bus passed a shopping center. At the far corner of the parking lot was a bank. Sitting in front of the bank was a police car.

"Okay. Let's get off here and stop at that store," replied Alicia. Julian stood and rang the bell. As Alicia stepped off the bus, she ran her fingers along her waist until she felt the gun handle.

"Do you want to pick up a pizza while we're out?" asked Julian.

But Alicia didn't hear his words. Her eyes focused on the police car sitting in front of the bank. Suddenly, the door opened, and two police officers climbed out. They looked towards the two teenagers but seemed more concerned with smoking their cigarettes. One of the police officers laughed loudly and took a drag on his cigarette.

"Well? Are you in the mood for pizza or not?" continued Julian. Finally, Alicia heard him.

"Oh. I don't know. You decide," Alicia responded. Julian looked over at the police and then turned back to Alicia.

"You want to go to another spot?" he asked her softly.

"What makes you ask that?" she asked. Julian nodded in the direction of the police.

When the two reached the center of the large parking lot, Alicia stopped walking.

"Julian, did you mean what you told me?"

"About what?"

"About being with me forever. Did you mean it?"

"Sure, I did. Why do you ask?"

Alicia stuck her hands underneath the hoodie and grabbed the gun's handle.

"Remember when I told you that one day you would have to prove your love to me?"

Julian moved closer to her.

"What is this, Alicia? What's going on?"

"Do you remember, yes or no?"

"Yeah, I remember."

"Well, today is that day. Prove it!"

"How?"

"Prove it!"

Alicia started walking quickly in the direction of the police car.

"Hey! Officer!" she yelled.

The two police officers lifted themselves off the car's hood and stood alert.

"Do either of you know Michael Kelly?" she continued.

"Who?" asked one of the officers.

"Michael Kelly. He's paralyzed. Paralyzed by one of your police officers."

Julian's eyes widened, and he grabbed Alicia by the arm.

"Hey! What are you doing? Stop!"

But Alicia wouldn't stop. Her blood burned like lava in her veins. She was going to have her say, no matter what.

"Excuse us, Officers. My girlfriend confused you with someone else," Julian tried to explain. But Alicia remained focused. She yanked her arm away from Julian and moved within a few feet of the officers.

"You don't know Michael Kelly?" she asked again. Although the two police officers towered over the small girl like giants, Alicia wasn't afraid. She felt drenched in anticipation of what she was about to do. Her heartbeat was calm, and her hands were steady.

"Isn't it too late for you kids to be out? It's Sunday," exclaimed one of the Officers. "Shouldn't you be home getting ready for school?"

"Fucking kids," snapped one of the officers. He took a deep drag on his cigarette and glared at the two teenagers standing before them. After tossing the cigarette butt onto the asphalt, he turned away to walk to the passenger side of the car. As soon as he took one step, Alicia yanked the gun from her waist. She put the barrel underneath the policeman's chin and pulled the trigger. There was a loud pop, and the man's skull exploded, shooting blood all over the car.

"Oh shit!" screamed Julian. After seeing the officer fall, he searched the darkness until he found Alicia's face. Her eyes were wild with pleasure as she took in the bloody scene, an evil smile on her face. Julian stumbled backward and fell to the ground.

"Son of a bitch!" screamed the other policeman. The cursing of the officer snapped Alicia back to reality, and she moved towards the other officer. The officer grabbed the holster of his gun and attempted to pull out his weapon, but Alicia was like black lightning in the shadows of the parking lot. Before he could lift the gun out, Alicia was behind him with her gun pointed at the base of his back. She quickly pulled the trigger twice and watched as the officer fell to the ground.

"Aaaagh! I can't feel my legs!" he yelled, squirming on the pavement. The policeman reached behind his back and pulled back two hands covered in blood.

"You...fucking...bitch..." he continued as he struggled to breathe. Alicia moved closer to the incapacitated man and held the barrel of the gun over his head.

"Don't...do it. I have a kid," said the officer, staring into the weapon barrel. But the power of the moment had overcome Alicia. She was no longer a child. She had become all that every wronged person wished to be. She was revenge.

"Alicia, what have you done?" asked Julian after climbing back to his feet. Quickly, he searched the parking lot to see if anyone was around.

"Don't do it, Alicia. Let's get out of here," said Julian as he moved closer to her.

"We can't."

"Let's go before someone sees us!"

"You said my name. He knows who I am."

"Alicia! Don't!"

"You said you loved me."

"What?"

"You said you would always be there for me."

"We don't have time for this shit! Let's go!"

Alicia lowered the weapon and turned to face Julian.

"Here," she said, holding out the weapon to Julian. "You finish him."

"Finish him?"

"Prove you love me."

Julian backed away from the weapon.

"I'm not going to fucking kill him."

"Do it!"

"Fuck you! I never agreed to this!"

Alicia righted the handgun and pointed it at Julian.

"So, you're no different than these pieces of shit."

Alicia took a step closer to Julian.

"You either kill him, or I kill you."

"Alicia, how can you do this?"

"Stop fucking around! It's him or you!"

Julian slowly took the weapon from Alicia's hand. He moved closer to the police officer.

"Please...I have a family..." the officer begged. Julian could feel his heart pounding through his clothes. He licked his lips and lowered the weapon to the officer's face.

"Do it," said Alicia.

Julian looked at Alicia and put his finger on the trigger. Suddenly, he sprinted past her, threw the gun into the darkness, and kept running without looking back. Alicia said nothing as she watched Julian's shadow disappear into the night. Calmly, she retrieved the gun from underneath a parked car. Alicia returned to the injured police officer lying in the shadows, who had stopped moving and was unconscious.

She lowered the weapon to his face and pulled the trigger. The officer's body jerked as the bullet entered his skull. After watching the blood pool around his head, Alicia walked over to the other officer lying on the ground. She lowered the gun close to his head and pulled the trigger. Moments later, she was running across the parking lot into the darkness.

40

The Dilemma

Julian was afraid to go home because he knew Alicia would be waiting for him. He was also scared of police swarms that would surely be on the street after discovering the dead police officers. Instead of getting on a bus, Julian cut through side streets. Whenever he saw a gas station or a grocery store, he went the opposite way, afraid of being recorded on a video camera or seen by an observant cashier. He cut through unfamiliar neighborhoods and tried to blend in with the darkness. After being spotted by an older man sitting on his porch smoking a pipe, Julian spotted an unlocked bike sitting in a yard. He stole it and took off riding along the roads until the roads became familiar. Julian whizzed along the streets until he finally arrived at the bridge leading to his school. He quickly rode underneath the bridge, pulling the bike into the underpass. Once there, Julian sat on the cold concrete and listened as the cars sped overhead.

When the sun came up, Julian was shivering. He cursed himself for not dressing warmer. Julian forgot that summer was rapidly changing to fall. On top of freezing in the morning air, he was also starving. He had decided to eat dinner with Alicia, but her antics made him completely forget his appetite.

"Alicia..." he whispered.

Julian was terrified of her. It wasn't just the fact that she'd held a gun to Julian's head and threatened to kill him. The most frightening aspect of Alicia was that he didn't know her. It was like she was another woman. The woman that he had seen in that parking lot attacked two police officers without remorse. Even as the officer had begged for his life and talked about his children, Alicia seemed to enjoy the man's anguish. There was nothing the man could have said to delay her wrath. Alicia was a monstrous murderer. She was cold, calculating, and damaged. He had to consider the fact that she could even be - evil.

"Maybe I should go to the cops," Julian said as he brushed dirt from his shoes. After all, she had killed the cops, not him. But after a few moments, Julian decided against that. Who would believe it? Alicia was a tiny girl. No one would ever guess that a small girl could do something so evil. Plus, they were both Black. It wouldn't matter which one of them shot the police officers. The cops would try to fry them both.

"And then there's the gun," whispered Julian.

Even though it was dark, he had recognized the weapon; it was his uncle's pistol from the backyard. Alicia had stolen it from him.

Julian lowered his head into his palms.

"I'm so fucking stupid!" he moaned. What did he expect from a kleptomaniac? Of course, she was going to take it.

By the time night arrived for the second time, Julian was so hungry that his hands were shaking. His head was throbbing, and he could barely think of anything but food.

"Man, fuck this."

Julian left the bike underneath the bridge and walked to the bus stop. After taking a few transfers, 2 hours later, he was at the front door of his apartment. Without looking around, he unlocked the door and went in.

Alicia wasn't there.

Julian entered the kitchen, grabbed a box of cereal from the cabinet, and gorged until his hunger eased a little. Next, he grabbed a frozen dinner and placed it in the oven. Julian entered the living room, grabbed the TV remote, and flopped on the sofa. As soon as he turned on the TV, the police murders' coverage leaped out at him. Julian sat entranced as the reporters talked about the crime. There were no witnesses and no fingerprints. The police were offering a $100,000 reward for information leading to the arrest of the suspects. Julian changed to another TV channel. One man had claimed that he'd seen a suspicious black man running through his neighborhood late at night. Police had questioned him, but he could not give them any information except for the man's height.

Finally, satisfied that the police didn't have his identity, Julian turned off the TV and showered. When he finished, he climbed into bed, closed his eyes, and fell asleep.

Suddenly, he was in the parking lot again. He could see the pale face of the police officer reaching up to him as Julian stood over him, watching him bleed.

"Help me...please...I have a family..." the man begged.

Suddenly, Alicia's face swung into view. Her eyes were glowing red, and thick, white foam was on the corners of her mouth. She grabbed Julian by the throat and slammed the gun into his chest.

"Take it! Kill him!" she demanded.

"No! I don't want to!" cried Julian.

"If you love me, you'll do it!" she hissed.

Suddenly, Julian had the gun in his hand. As if another person was controlling him, he aimed the weapon at the man's head.

"Do it, you fucking chicken shit!" the officer growled. He was no longer begging. Instead, his eyes were glowing red, and his body convulsed as if somebody possessed him. He was daring Julian to commit murder. Suddenly, Alicia started laughing, a deep demonic voice echoing inside her.

"If you love me, you'll do it!"

"No! I won't!"

"You will!"

There was a loud bang, and Julian looked down at his hands. He was holding the gun, covered in blood.

"Aaaaagh!"

Suddenly, Julian woke up in his bed, drenched in sweat. It was night, and the bedroom was black. He jumped out of bed and turned on the light. He immediately walked into the living room and turned on the TV. The first thing he saw was a reporter at the crime scene.

"Hello, Andrea. It was here at the West Dover Shopping Center where the grisly murders took place. On Sunday, a patron of Tilly's Convenience Store was driving through the parking lot toward the exit when he found the two officers unresponsive lying in the parking lot. So far, the police have no suspects or clues that could lead to an arrest. The Metro Police Department has agreed to increase the reward to $120,000 for information leading to the shooter's arrest or shooters involved in the officers' execution. Tons of leads are pouring in, but no arrests have been made."

Julian turned off the TV and slammed the remote on the floor.

"Crazy bitch!" he yelled. "I should turn her ass in."

Frustrated and scared, he gathered the remote pieces from the floor. Grateful that only the back of the TV remote that kept the batteries had popped off, Julian sat down and turned the television back on. He continued watching TV until the sun came up.

41

Living in Fear

Julian had to quit the football team. He had no choice. Julian could barely pay attention in class because he was exhausted. Every night, he stayed up late and was glued to the television, watching to see if the cops were closing in on him. Staying at home felt like the cops would burst into the apartment at any moment. Being in school was worse. Not only was he worried about the police, but he was also concerned that Alicia would sneak up behind him at the first opportunity.

Alicia was gone. She wasn't in her classes, and none of the people she spoke to regularly had seen her. Julian began to wonder if she'd killed herself. Julian had seen how people got pushed over the edge too many times in movies. It always ended with the crazy person taking their own life.

One day melted into the next until it was Friday again. Julian decided not to go to school that day but didn't stay home. Instead, he picked up a few extra work hours at the restaurant. Julian knew Alicia would eventually come looking for revenge. He needed to buy a gun.

Friday night, Julian returned to his apartment tired and smelling of seafood. He flopped down and turned on the TV. The murders' reporting had diminished, and most TV stations had returned to their regular programming. After watching for a few minutes, he went into the kitchen, made a bologna sandwich, and headed to the shower.

Julian dried himself off and wrapped himself in his towel. He walked into the bedroom. When he turned on the light, he almost fell.

Alicia was sitting on his bed!

"Don't bother running," she said while holding up the gun. Julian was terrified. Alicia's face was twitching as she looked at him.

"Look. I don't know what you want, but..." Julian said, holding up one hand while the other gripped his towel. Alicia stood up suddenly and kicked the dresser."

"You promised me! Do you remember that?"

"I know I did, but I never promised..."

"Promised what? Murder?"

"Yeah."

Alicia started crying.

"They took everything from me! I had to!"

"You could've found another way."

Alicia started to laugh.

"Found another way? How do you find a way to resurrect my daddy? You have a way to do that?"

Julian was silent. It was clear that any response he made would only anger Alicia more.

"Do you know what it's like for a little girl to surrender her life to pain? Do you know what that can do to a child? Do you know what it's like to smell your daddy's piss and shit day after day? To see the gaping hole in his fucking head made by some racist prick just for kicks?"

"Everyone has problems, Alicia."

Alicia ran up to Julian and smacked him in the face.

"Don't do that! Don't you fucking do that! You know what I went through was different. Hell, why am I even saying this to you? What you went through was different too!"

"Yeah, but I didn't kill two innocent people to solve my problems."

"I don't feel an ounce of remorse for those people. Maybe I didn't know them, but I didn't have to. They belonged to the same fucked up system that killed my dad. Guilt by association is enough for me."

Julian was getting angrier by the second.

"Why didn't you talk to me about this?"

"I did tell you! You weren't listening."

"Really? When the fuck was that? I deserved to know in advance if you were going to blow those officers' heads off."

"Maybe."

"Maybe? Are you fucking serious? If you loved me, you would've told me what you planned to do. Or, at the very least, you could've done it alone without including me in your sick act of revenge."

"I only did it because..."

"Because of what? You're selfish and no different than the assholes who hurt your father. You don't love me!"

Alicia ran to Julian and threw her arms around his neck.

"I do love you. Don't you see it? I didn't want to hide anything from you. You're the best thing that ever happened to me. I knew I would lose you if I told you what I planned to do. It was the only way to be sure you would be with me forever."

"That's selfish as fuck."

Alicia pushed Julian against the wall and returned to the room's other side.

"So, what do you want to do? Are we going to be together or not?"

"Be together?! You killed two cops! How is that even possible? If we escape the death penalty, they'll search for us for the rest of our lives!"

Alicia stuck her hands into her jacket.

"Are we together or not?"

Julian took notice of her hand in her jacket and froze. He was sure she had the gun.

"We're together...for now."

Alicia moved closer to him.

"Do you want to turn me in?"

Julian could see the same icy glare in Alicia's eyes that he'd seen on the night of the murders. He knew that if she thought he was going to turn her in, she would kill him.

"Baby...no. I want a way out of this mess."

Alicia removed her hand from her jacket and walked over to her boyfriend. She kissed him hard on the lips and grabbed him by the throat.

"You promised me you would never leave. Do you want to leave me?"

Julian closed his eyes as she ran her tongue along his lips. Before the murders, Alicia's domination would have Julian begging for punishment. But this time was different, and Julian was terrified. Alicia wasn't the person kissing him. The person dominating him now was a monster.

"Touch me," Alicia instructed. Julian lifted his hand and caressed her face. Suddenly, Alicia slapped him across the face so hard that he saw flashing lights.

"When I tell you to do something, you do it!" she yelled. Julian could taste the blood in his mouth. Nothing about this moment was erotic. A monster trapped Julian in a world of pain.

"Lose the towel and go lay on the bed!" Alicia demanded. Julian objected.

"Baby...we don't have time for this. Shouldn't we be..."

This time, Alicia hit him in the mouth with a fist. Julian almost fell to the floor.

"What the fuck is wrong with you?" he yelled. Alicia smiled a wicked smile. She took off her pants and shirt.

"This isn't what you wanted?"

Julian was angry now.

"No! Fuck, no!"

"You sure?"

Alicia pulled the gun out of the pile of clothes on the floor.

"Now, hold on, Alicia. You're taking this shit too far."

"Stop being a pussy!"

The anger boiled over in Julian. He hit Alicia in the face with his fist. She stumbled back and started laughing.

"I'm not playing this fucking game with you anymore!"

Alicia stood up and walked over to Julian.

"Come here, baby."

Alicia rubbed Julian's arm and pulled him close.

"Do you want to leave me?"

Julian could see that she was still holding the gun, but the anger within him was too intense.

"Yes! This relationship is over!"

Alicia lowered her head in defeat.

"Okay. If this is what you want, I'll go."

Suddenly, she lifted her head to look into Julian's eyes. Without warning, she struck him in the head with the butt of the gun. Julian fell on the bed, unconscious.

42

Strawberry Nights

Alicia woke up in the middle of the night, cold. Although she was under a blanket, the chill in the room felt like icy fingertips crawling up her exposed legs. Alicia climbed out of bed and checked the windows; they were closed and locked. She looked at her boyfriend; although he seemed to sleep soundly, his lips trembled. Alicia covered his body with the blanket before going to the closet. After fumbling around amongst the clutter of disorganization, she located one of Julian's oversized sweatshirts. She put it on and stepped out of the room into the hallway.

The hallway's temperature was the opposite of the bedroom. Instead of being cold, the hallway was so hot that Alicia looked around to ensure the house was not on fire. She closed the bedroom door behind her and turned on the hall light to look at the thermostat.

"Seventy degrees?" Alicia asked incredulously. "Maybe it's broken."

She lowered the thermostat to 60 degrees and wiped the sweat from her brow. Unable to stand the heat in the hallway, Alicia removed the sweatshirt she had just put on and walked into the kitchen to get a drink of cold water. She opened the refrigerator and stood, letting the cold air envelope her sweaty, naked body. Alicia smiled and breathed deeply. The refrigerator mist reminded her of her cool summer evenings with her dad. She could still hear how they had laughed as they splashed across the sidewalk on their way home. Finally, Alicia opened her eyes and looked for a glass. When she couldn't find one, she lifted the plastic container to her parched lips and gulped until she had her fill.

"Come walk with me," whispered a voice outside the kitchen door. Alicia shut the refrigerator door and walked to the backdoor. When she opened it, a dark shadow was standing in the center of the yard. Although she couldn't see the shadow's face, Alicia knew who it was.

"Daddy. I was waiting for you."

Alicia walked out of the apartment into the backyard. The shadow disappeared and then reappeared further away from her. If she stepped in the shadow's direction, it moved one step away.

"Stop running away from me, Daddy."

Suddenly, the shadow stopped evading. It rose high in the air, hovering just above Alicia's head. The girl extended her hands to touch the shadow; her hands moved through it like water, making Alicia feel warm and cold at once like being frozen in the middle of a burning July day.

"I did it, Daddy. I got revenge."

You must leave.

"Leave?"

He will abandon you. He will bring the police to you.

"Julian loves me. I know it."

He will call the police.

"But I know him. He wouldn't do that."

Search your heart. You know Julian is searching for a way to betray you.

"No, Daddy. You're mistaken. I will prove it."

Only a fool believes there is a cool breeze in hell.

"What if I take him to her?"

He will fail you.

"He won't."

Suddenly, the shadow began glowing a bright red.

They will come to you. It would be best if you had weapons—much more.

"I know. Where can I find some guns? How?"

The gun shop. At night. Steal them as you have stolen them before.

"I will take him to her. As a test. You will see."

The shadow rose into the sky and disappeared. Alicia raised her hands to the sky.

"Daddy! Come back!" she whispered over and over. But the shadow was gone. Sobbing, Alicia returned to the apartment. She put on Julian's sweatshirt again and crept out into the night. About an hour later, she returned with a pocket full of bullets.

"Daddy. Are you there?" she asked. But there was no answer. Tired and deflated, she returned to the bedroom.

43

Blueberry Nights

Julian drifted in and out of consciousness. One moment, everything was black, and the next moment, he was lying in bed next to Alicia. Each time he woke up, a nude Alicia was above him with a cold towel, wiping his head and talking to him as if he were awake.

"Relax. I'm here. Don't worry. I'll take care of you..."

"There are others like us. Abused, neglected, and left to die in this hell. So many of us. I see them walking through the hallways at school: girls with black eyes, boys with sad faces and bruised bodies, terrified of the world. I had to stand up for Daddy. If not me, then who would do it? And the funny part about all this? Everyone will look at me as the devil. I'd be just another crazy-ass girl who lost all her marbles. Even you think I'm nuts. All of you will say I went too far. But look what they did to my Daddy. I will find them. I'll show them and murder them. I loved my Daddy, and my Dad loved me. What right does evil have to destroy love without consequence?"

"...tired of being hurt. I'm invisible to the world. Nobody sees what they did to Daddy and me. Nobody cared. I'm so tired of this place. I want to feel more than pain..."

"When we make love, and I put my fingernails into your throat, I feel you...your pain. I feel what the lady did to you when she stole your innocence. And now your soul is twisted. Now, you crave pain and love at once. When I slap you and scratch your skin until it bleeds, I feel pieces of my soul melting away. Pain is like a virus. It infects all who are vulnerable. I sacrificed my body for you to show you that I am with you. This fight is a battle for both of us. Maybe we are just in different places. I've chosen to attack my pain directly while you have yet to confront yours. But the day will come when you must be strong enough to kill the pain. I want you to ride this wave with me. See beyond what they tell you. Accept the world they've given to us and use it to kill them..."

Julian woke up with a pounding headache in the middle of the night. He sat up in bed and looked around. Alicia was gone. Though barely able to stand up, he stumbled out of his bedroom and down the hall into the bathroom. Unable to steady himself, Julian urinated all over the toilet and floor. On his way back to the bedroom, he saw a shadow standing at the far end of the hallway. Julian stumbled towards it with both arms holding himself up, inching along the wall. When he arrived in the kitchen, the backdoor was wide open. As he stumbled over to close the door, Julian spotted the silhouette of a nude female standing in the middle of his backyard. Julian shook his head and rubbed his eyes. When he opened his eyes again, the woman was gone. Dazed and confused, Julian stumbled back to bed.

44

The Visit

When Julian woke up again, the sun was shining on his face. He squinted and turned away from the sun. His head was still throbbing, but it wasn't as bad as before. Suddenly, the smell of bacon filled his nose. Julian thought he was just hungry and imagining things until he heard a female voice singing in the kitchen. He sat up and looked around the bedroom. Suddenly, the bedroom door swung open, and Alicia walked in carrying a tray of food.

"Good morning, sleepyhead. I thought you were going to sleep for the whole day. I made you some breakfast. You'll need all your strength before we get on the road."

"Get on the road?"

Alicia smiled and put her hands on her hips.

"Don't tell me you forgot."

"Forgot what?"

"Today is the day we visit your mom."

Julian looked surprised. Alicia didn't think he would introduce her to his mother after all she had done.

"Um, I think we need to delay that. It's not the right time."

"Don't be silly. Your mom's in prison. Why wouldn't it be the right time? She's probably dying to see you. You haven't been for a few weeks, right?"

"Alicia! You killed two fucking cops, and now you want to enter the belly of the beast? What are you thinking? If the cops find out you're the murderer they're looking for, we're dead!"

"We're going."

"I'm not going. Not after what you did."

Alicia turned to leave and paused at the door.

"After you finish your breakfast, we're heading out. It'll be fun, baby. Don't worry."

As soon as Alicia was gone, Julian put the food tray on the ground. He stood up and walked to the mirror to look at himself.

"Fuck!" he said. There was a massive bump on his head with a deep cut in the center. He touched it gently with his finger and winced in pain.

"Alicia!" he whispered. He sat down on the bed, grabbed his blood-stained pillow, and tossed it across the room.

"This can't go on."

Julian finally reached his limit. He knew he had to turn Alicia in. Julian only had to find the right time and place. He sat in silence for a few minutes to think about his predicament. Finally, he stood up and went to the closet to get dressed. Visiting his mom would be the perfect place to turn Alicia in; she wouldn't have a gun, she couldn't get violent, and there would be no room for her escape.

After getting dressed, Julian ate the bacon and eggs on the tray. Reenergized, he walked into the kitchen and kissed Alicia on the cheek as she washed dishes.

"You're right. We should visit Mom. She's probably lonely since the last time I went there."

"Plus, it's only right for you to introduce me. After all, you met my dad. I should meet your mom."

Julian smiled and walked back to the bedroom.

"I'm sorry, Alicia. We can't do this anymore," he said as he shut the bedroom door. This moment would be the last time he was going to see Alicia.

45

Crazy Days

When Julian and Alicia arrived at the prison entrance, they exited the bus and walked across the parking lot to the main door. Alicia removed a brown paper bag from underneath her shirt and dropped it in the garbage before entering the gates.

"What was that?" asked Julian.

"Oh, nothing. Just some personal girl stuff I needed to get rid of," replied Alicia.

But Julian knew better. That was the gun. He had to find a way to turn her in without her returning to the parking lot. The two teenagers went through the security checkpoint. After being searched, they passed through the metal detectors and entered the building.

The guards took the visitors to a waiting area to have their names confirmed for visitation. Once Julian and Alicia had their names confirmed, the guards moved them into the main visiting area. They sat at one of the metal tables and looked at the door, waiting for Julian's mother to come out. It wasn't long until the correctional officers led her out. As soon as she reached their table, Julian's mother stared at him in disbelief.

"What the hell, Julian?"

Julian's mom sat down at the table and touched her son on the head.

"I hit my head on the mirror this morning."

"What the hell were you doing? That's one hell of a bump."

"It's nothing, mom."

"Does it hurt?"

"Of course."

"You've always been a bit accident-prone. Remember when you fell down the stairs when you went trick-or-treating?"

Julian sighed.

"Not that story again."

"You're always getting hurt."

Julian's mother turned to Alicia.

"And you must be my son's girlfriend, Alicia. How are you?"

Alicia smiled politely at the woman.

"It's such a pleasure to meet you. I've heard so much about you."

"Well, seeing as I'm in this hell hole, I know you didn't hear all good things about me."

"I think I heard mostly good things. The way you put that bitch in her grave when she fucked with your child, that shit was legendary. Truly admirable. I mean that."

Julian's mother looked confused. She looked from Alicia to her son before responding.

"Well, I wouldn't say it's legendary. After all, that woman's family suffered just as much as mine did. But some pains are unavoidable."

The group sat in silence for a few moments.

"So...how old are you, Alicia?"

"Sixteen."

"What do you plan on doing when you graduate?"

"I don't know. I haven't decided yet."

"Well, my son plans on going to college. Hopefully, on a football scholarship."

Alicia started giggling.

"I'm sorry. Am I missing the joke?" asked Julian's mom.

"I don't know how he's going to get a football scholarship if he quit playing football," replied Alicia.

"What?"

Suddenly, Julian's mother was alarmed.

"Julian, did you stop playing football?"

Julian reached under the table and squeezed Alicia's leg.

"Not exactly."

"Not exactly? What does that mean? You play the game, or you don't."

"I decided to take this year off. I can always try out for the team when I go to college?"

"Boy! Did you lose your fucking mind? How are you going to get to college? I don't have enough money to pay for that."

Suddenly, Alicia spoke up.

"They murdered my dad."

Julian's mother stared at Alicia in disbelief.

"Excuse me. What?"

"Yeah. The police attacked Daddy while I was in the car. They crippled him. He died recently."

"Shit!"

A distant look came into Alicia's eyes, and she squeezed Julian's hand. Julian's mother noticed the look and reached across the table.

"Honey, are you okay?" asked Julian's mother. "Maybe you should go home."

"I wish I were as strong as you. I want to avenge my dad, but..."

Julian interrupted.

"Hey, baby. Now isn't the right time for that subject. We're sitting in prison with police all around us."

"My father's dead, Julian. Killed by fucking police officers. Do you expect me to bite my tongue for their benefit?"

This time, Julian's mother interrupted.

"Julian's right, Alicia. While I'm sympathetic to what happened to your dad, now isn't the time to be talking about..."

"I want to be like you, Ms. Williamson. I want to put a gun into a cop's mouth and..."

"Alicia, would you please excuse us for a few minutes? I need to talk with my son."

Alicia stared at the woman without blinking.

"No!"

"No?"

"You're going to talk about me, so why must I leave?"

Julian's mother's chest puffed up in anger.

"Little girl, if you don't get your ass up from this table, I'll..."

"Mom! Stop! Alicia, can you please excuse us?"

"I'm not going anywhere."

"Alicia! Stop!"

Suddenly, the officer walked over to the table.

"Is there a problem here?"

"No, there's not a problem. Alicia needs to wait outside while I speak with my son."

Alicia's eyes widened when she saw the officer's badge. Suddenly, she thrust the chair back, stood up, and pointed her finger at the officer.

"I'll go. But don't you put your fucking hands on me!"

Alicia walked to the exit and paused at the door.

"Hurry up, Julian. I'll be waiting out front!" she said and stormed out of the room.

As soon as she was gone, Julian's mother whispered to her son.

"Julian, what have you gotten yourself into?"

"I know, mom. I know."

"Is she crazy or something?"

"I don't think she's crazy. But she's hurt."

"It was her that hit you on the head, wasn't it?"

Julian lowered his head in shame.

"She didn't do it to harm me, Mom. Trust me. It's more complex than that. She's a good person. But the things she had to endure were so unfair."

"Well... one thing's for sure. Alicia's a complex child."

"I know, mom. I was thinking about reporting her. You know, to get her some help. "

"To whom? The police?"

"Yeah."

"No way, Julian. If she's crazy, reporting her to the cops will make her batshit. These cages and walls could make anyone go crazy. Nobody deserves that. Even I can see she's got a ton of issues because of the way her father died. But jail would drive her insane. That's a death sentence for sure."

"Then what should I do? I'm running out of options on how to deal with her."

Suddenly, a corrections officer moved closer to their table. Julian's mother changed the subject.

"Well, I was going to tell you later, but I may as well tell you now. I'll be out of here in 2 weeks."

"Mom! That's awesome! How did you pull that off?"

"Good behavior."

"Uncle Dex hasn't come home yet."

"Yeah. Your uncle's looking at a long time in prison. No parole."

"It looks like it'll be just you and me."

"Same as it ever was."

Satisfied with the conversation, the correctional officer moved away from their table.

Julian's mother leaned in close to him.

"Julian. I'm not always going to be here to fight your battles. You need to stand up and be a man. She's not the kind of girl I had in mind for you, but it's not my decision. Do you love her?"

"Yes, mom. I think I do."

"Do you love her enough to help when she's most vulnerable?"

Julian took a deep breath and exhaled.

"There are things you don't know, mom."

"That's not what I asked, Julian."

Julian thought about the question before responding.

"Yes. I think I can stand with Alicia."

"Every damaged item isn't trash, Julian. One thing I learned in this place is that life is about you. It isn't about your friends, your family, or what society wants you to be. It's about what you want for yourself."

"I know, mom."

"Do you? Because in this situation, you only have two options. Either love her no matter what happens or get rid of her. There are no in-betweens."

"I know, mom. I know."

"Stop saying that!"

Julian's mom poked Julian in the chest with her index finger.

"If you don't know what you want, your life is over. Stop being an indecisive pussy! I won't fight any more battles for you. It's time to grow up."

Another guard walked over and interrupted them.

"Times up, Chris. Let's go."

"Yeah. Time's up, Julian. What are you going to do? What are you going to make of yourself?"

Julian's mother stood up and hugged her son.

"Take care of yourself. I'll see you in two weeks. Remember. If I were you, I would get rid of Alicia. But moms have been known to be wrong from time to time. Fight for her if you think the love is worth the effort."

Julian walked across the room and out the door. As soon as he left the building, he saw Alicia sitting on the sidewalk. She was holding the paper bag in her hand.

"Let's go," he said. The two walked up the sidewalk to the bus stop.

46

Prove Yourself Again

Alicia and Julian were silent on their way back to his apartment. Alicia sat, staring out the window for most of the trip back, and Julian looked around the bus to avoid making eye contact with the girl sitting beside him. When the bus pulled into its first transfer station, Alicia finally spoke.

"I need to stop by Natalie's house," she said quietly.

"For what?" asked Julian. Alicia could tell he was annoyed. Still, she continued.

"I need some money for expenses. I can't have you paying for everything for me."

"How much longer do you plan on staying with me?"

"Why? Are you trying to get rid of me?"

The question seemed like she dared him to say he wanted to break up. He steered her line of questioning to something else.

"You haven't been home in a while. Is Natalie still paying the rent?"

"I think so, but I haven't spoken to her for a while."

"Don't you think you need to have a conversation with her? I mean, she's your guardian."

"Well, that's part of the reason for my visit."

"Okay. Fine."

After transferring buses, the two teenagers traveled for another two hours before reaching Natalie's condo.

"Good. Natalie's car is here. She's home," said Alicia as she and Julian walked off the bus. Julian was nervous about this visit. He remembered all the things Alicia had told him about her guardian. She had a deep hatred for the woman because of the injury to her father. Julian wasn't comfortable with randomly showing up at a stranger's house with a stone-cold murderer in his midst.

Alicia rang the doorbell and waited. Seconds later, a voice rang out.

"Who is it?"

"Hi, Natalie. It's me. Alicia. I brought my boyfriend to meet you."

"Alicia?"

There was a delay before the woman started to unlock the door. Natalie peered out the door through a crack before finally opening it completely.

"What are you doing here? It's kind of late for a visit. No?"

Finally, Natalie opened the door all the way.

"I just wanted you to meet my boyfriend," explained Alicia.

Julian extended his hand.

"Hi, I'm Julian. Nice to meet you."

Natalie looked suspiciously at both teenagers. Reluctantly, she opened the door wide.

"I've seen you at school. Come in. Come in."

Once inside, Alicia breathed deeply.

"Is that banana bread I smell?"

"Yes. Good nose. I'll get you guys a slice," said Natalie as she stood to walk to the kitchen. "Alicia, can you give me a hand?"

Alicia stood and followed her into the kitchen. As Natalie grabbed the saucers from the cabinet, she laid into Alicia.

"What do you have to say for yourself?"

"What do you mean?"

"What do I mean? On the night I let you stay here, you destroyed my cake and messed up my table."

Alicia turned away from Natalie.

"I was dealing with a lot of emotion. I didn't know what I was doing."

"I figured that much. That's why I've given you several days to think about things. Is that the reason you haven't been attending school?"

"How do you know?"

"Did you think the school wasn't going to call me?"

"I've just been trying to handle things without Daddy."

Suddenly, Alicia started crying. Natalie placed the knife on the counter and turned to embrace the young girl.

"I know. I know. This whole situation is so fucked up."

"What am I going to do without my Daddy?"

"It'll be difficult. But no matter what, I'm here to help you."

Alicia lifted her head and stared into Natalie's eyes.

"Do you mean that?"

Natalie wiped her tears away and kissed her cheeks.

"I mean it."

"Seriously?

"Yes."

"Then I need you to tell me something."

"What is it?"

"Tell me the man's name."

"What, man?"

"The manager. The man that called the cops on my Dad."

Natalie let go of Alicia and backed away.

"Why do you want his name?"

"Because I do."

"That's not going to bring your father back."

"So, you won't give me his name?"

"No. That's something I can't be a part of."

"So, you're not on my side. You're on that prick's side."

"I'm sure you don't mean that."

"Did you stop him? Or were you more concerned with protecting your family from a lawsuit?"

"No, but..."

Alicia walked close to the counter and picked up the knife.

"Do you want to know something? I've always hated you. You're as fake as a three-dollar bill."

Natalie noticed the knife in the girl's hand and started inching away.

"Yeah, you helped us for all these years. I give you credit for that. But you don't get an award for it. How could a racist son of a bitch like that get hired in your family's store? Someone behind the scenes harbored those same racist beliefs."

"I can see you're upset. Maybe we should get you some help."

"I need help. Me? You're sitting there trying to protect the identity of a man who was the cause of my father's death. And I need help?"

"Everyone needs help from time to time, Alicia."

Alicia gripped the knife tightly in her hand and moved closer to Natalie. Nervously, the large woman looked from the girl's hands to her wide eyes.

"What?" asked Alicia as she held up the weapon. "Are you afraid of me because I'm holding this knife?"

"Alicia...please...you can't...."

Alicia flipped the knife over so that the handle pointed towards Natalie. With her bare hand, Alicia squeezed the blade until blood started dripping from her hand.

"The big white security guard is afraid of the little black girl. Isn't that funny?"

"Alicia, your hand!"

"Here. Take the knife."

Blood was pouring from Alicia's hand now. Natalie took the weapon's handle in one hand and tried to lift the girl's fingers from the blade. As she lifted the first finger, Natalie grimaced in disgust. The knife was deep in her flesh. But Alicia didn't flinch. She continued staring at Natalie's face as if in a trance. Finally, she let go of the blade, and Natalie rushed to the sink to grab a towel.

"Here. Wrap your hand with this."

Alicia grabbed the towel and wrapped her hand in it. Suddenly, she ran into the living room.

"Come on. We've got to go."

"Holy shit! What happened to your hand?"

"She cut me."

"What? Why?"

Natalie walked into the room, holding the bloody knife.

"Let me take you to the hospital."

Julian was confused. He didn't know what had happened.

"What did you do to her?"

"Who? Me? Nothing. She cut herself."

Julian walked over to Alicia and unwrapped her hand from the towel. As soon as he did, blood began pouring from the wound.

"We've got to go. Now. You'll lose that finger if we don't get help."

Julian opened the door and gently grabbed his girlfriend by her arm.

"Come on. Let's go."

Alicia turned to Natalie.

"This is your last chance. What's his name?"

Natalie stood staring at the teenagers, not saying a word.

"Hey. We don't have time for this. You're losing a lot of blood," said Julian as he tried to push Alicia out the door. But Alicia wouldn't budge. She stood frozen, waiting for Natalie to speak.

"I told you no."

"Then, you die."

Startled, Julian moved away from Alicia.

"What the hell is going on?" he asked. Natalie's eyes began filling with tears.

"I shouldn't have left you alone in that apartment. I should've been there with you."

"It's too late for that now, isn't it?"

"We can get you some help. I'll drive you."

Alicia reached into the back of her pants and pulled out the handgun. She pushed Julian aside and walked up to Natalie.

"You're going to kill me? After all the stuff I did for you and your father?"

"It's his name or yours."

Alicia aimed the gun in Natalie's face.

"Okay! Okay! His name is Bob. Bob Pritchard."

"Where is he? What's his address?"

"182 Mulberry Street."

Alicia lowered the gun and turned to look at her boyfriend, who was standing beside the door.

"Do you know where that is, Julian?"

"Yes. But why do you want to go there?"

"Are you with me?" she asked. Nervously, Julian looked from the gun to Natalie. Afraid of her response, he replied the only way he could.

"Yes."

Suddenly, she raised the gun and pulled the trigger. A red mist sprayed from behind Natalie's head, and she fell to the ground.

"What the fuck!" yelled Julian. "Why did you have to do that?"

"She cut me. You saw that. It's her knife, in her hand, with my blood."

Suddenly, Natalie started gurgling and moaning. She wasn't dead.

Alicia held out the weapon to Julian.

"Here. You finish that bitch."

"What? No fucking way!"

"Do it! Don't you dare turn your back on me now!"

"Fuck you, Alicia. I'm not killing her."

Alicia held the gun up to Julian's face.

"Do it."

"Fuck you."

Alicia let out a sigh and shook her head.

"Fine. Your choice."

Julian closed his eyes and prepared for death. But there was no loud noise. Instead, all he heard was a metallic click. He opened his eyes and saw Alicia struggling with the weapon. Julian saw his opportunity. He pushed the girl so hard that she flew across the room into the wall, knocking Alicia unconscious. After ensuring she was still breathing, Julian picked up the phone and dialed 911.

"Hello, 911. What's your emergency?" asked the operator. Julian lowered the phone to the table and backed out of the front door. He ran away from the house after gently closing the door behind him.

After a few minutes, Alicia moaned and opened her eyes.

"Shit!" she cursed. Her head was throbbing. After noticing her hand was numb, she lifted it to look at it. Alicia unwrapped her hand and tossed the bloody towel to the floor. She stood up and looked around, but Julian was gone. Suddenly, she heard a faint whisper.

"Alicia...Alicia..."

She walked over to Natalie and stood over her. Although the bullet had pierced her skull, she was still alive. The whites of her eyes were red with blood; a pool was forming underneath her head.

"I'm sorry, Alicia. You're right about me. Yes, I moved into your house to minimize the damage to my family. Mom lost Dad. It was the only thing I could think of to protect her. I'm sorry," whispered Natalie as she coughed and wheezed. "Get on the phone. Tell them there's been an accident. I won't blame you. I'll say it was something else."

Alicia looked around until she spotted the telephone receiver on the table. She walked over to it and was about to grab it when she heard a voice call out to her.

Finish it! She tried to protect the man that hurt me!

Alicia stumbled backward and pressed both her palms against her temple.

I told you he would betray you. I warned you. Now you know what you must do.

"No more...please," cried Alicia as she sat on the sofa. Her head was throbbing, the voice echoing inside her head like voices in a cave.

You must finish it; they're coming for you! He called them before he ran.

Natalie coughed again.

"Alicia...call for help."

Alicia stood up from the sofa and walked over to Natalie.

"You shut up! It's all your fault! You made me what I am!"

"I love you, Alicia. Do you hear me? I love you."

Alicia shook her head rapidly.

"Stop saying that! You don't! You're just like them! You held me hostage to protect your family. You could've saved Daddy! Do you understand that? He should be here with the money we would've won from the courts!"

"No..."

"You don't know that! Daddy could've been saved! Maybe they could've found what was wrong. But your greed fucked us over! You killed him!"

The voice in her head grew louder. Alicia blinked her eyes furiously as she struggled to understand what was happening. Still, the words were heavy in her head. It yelled louder. The voice was like thunder trapped in a tunnel.

Kill her! Kill her! Kill her!

"I love you, Alicia," gasped Natalie.

Kill her now! Now! Do it!

Alicia's eyes fell on the bloody knife that Natalie had been holding. She walked over and grabbed it.

"I'm sorry. I have to."

Natalie's eyes widened when she saw the knife in Alicia's hands. She closed her eyes and spoke.

"I know you don't believe me, but I love you."

Alicia grabbed a handful of Natalie's hair and pulled back far enough to expose her neck. With one rough motion, she ran the blade across Natalie's throat. There was a gurgling sound as air and blood escaped her throat at once. Natalie squeezed her eyes shut. Her body jerked, and her mouth opened, searching for breath only to have it stolen by the gaping wound in her neck. Soon, the muscles relaxed in her face, and a final breath escaped her. She was gone.

Alicia stood above Natalie's body, crying and laughing simultaneously. Madness had overcome her. She began yanking at her hair and cursing aloud.

"Kill me, you fuckers! Do it! I'm here waiting for you son-of-a-bitches! Finish the job! Come on! I'm here!"

You must find him! Find him before he reaches the police! Find him and kill him!

The sound of approaching sirens began to cry out. Alicia looked around until she found the gun lying on the floor. She grabbed it and tucked the knife into her jeans.

"You let me down again. I'll find you. I'll fix this."

She looked out the front door to see if any cop cars were visible. No one had arrived, but the sirens were getting louder and louder. She took off, running across the street and into the forest on the opposite side of the road.

47

The Sellout & The Murderer

Julian stood on the opposite side of the street, staring at the police precinct. Hidden in the forest's darkness, he saw police officers moving from room to room with purpose. He imagined they were all trying to find out who killed the two police officers.

"Come on. You've got to do it. This shit has gone too far," Julian whispered from the darkness. He was pushing himself to take the final step he knew he had to endure. Julian had to go into the police station and end the madness. If he didn't, his story would surely end the same way Alicia's life would, with dozens of cops surrounding him, pumping his body full of lead. Maybe it was a proper ending to both their stories. Emotionally, they were both irreparably damaged. Possibly, in a different life, they could repair their broken spirits. But in this life, they were twins trapped in various levels of hell. Maybe they both deserved to die.

Suddenly, a large group of police officers started pouring out of the building. They all hopped into their vehicles and raced away into the night.

"Natalie," Julian whispered. He hoped Alicia was still there when they arrived, but deep down, he knew the truth. She had probably fled the scene before the cops came. Although Alicia was crazy, Julian knew Alicia was brilliant. It took an intelligent and strong spirit to survive in this world. And she was probably coming for him.

After the last car had pulled out of the precinct parking lot, Julian decided to enter the building. He was about to exit the forest when he heard tree branches snap behind him.

"Make one move, and I'll blow your fucking head off."

He turned around and peered into the forest.

"Alicia?"

"You know who it is."

"Look. I don't want any problems. I want this to end."

"Oh, it'll end all right. Make no mistake about that."

Alicia emerged from behind a tree and walked closer to Julian.

"You called the cops, didn't you?"

"What else could I do? You've killed three people."

"I loved you. I gave you pieces of me. Whatever you needed to be whole, I gave it to you. Why couldn't you do the same for me?"

A thought entered Julian's head. At that moment, he saw Alicia for who she was. She was a victim stumbling through the darkness, trying to protect herself. Julian moved towards Alicia.

"Look. Maybe we can fix things between us. I was scared. But I'm not now. I see your point of view. I'm on your side now."

Julian wasn't sure if his words were right or wrong. All he knew was that Alicia only did what she could to survive.

"Love isn't some ball you can play with and toss away at your convenience. You're with me, or I'm alone in this hell. There is no in-between."

Julian smiled. Although the words were slightly different, Alicia's words were almost identical in sentiment to what his mother had spoken to him when he'd last seen her.

"I know, baby. You have to believe me. I see you now."

"Do you? Really? Because I can't see shit. I'm lost and don't know what to do next."

"Saying I love you won't fix things. I know."

"Whatever you do, don't say that shit to me."

"But I can say that I understand. I do. And if you want to get past the pain, we could help each other."

Alicia took a step back into the darkness.

"You sack of shit. You're trying to play on my emotions like I'm some soft-ass, ditsy kid. Fuck you."

"No. That's not it."

"Yeah? Then why are we standing across the street from a police station?"

"Because I'm just as lost as you are. Can't you see? We were supposed to be together."

Alicia lowered the weapon and backed away from Julian.

"Go ahead. Turn me in."

Julian looked puzzled. He could tell by her eyes that Alicia was up to something.

"No. I don't want to. Let's go to my place and figure something out."

Alicia raised the weapon again and cocked it.

"I said go. Tell the police what I did."

"No. There's a better way for us to solve this."

"You have 5 seconds to turn around and run towards that building. If you don't, I'll put a bullet in your head right here."

"Come on. You don't have to do this."

"5...4...3...2."

"Okay! Okay! I'm going."

Julian turned away from Alicia and walked out of the forest. As he crossed the street, heading to the police parking lot, he turned back to see if Alicia was still watching him. She was gone.

Julian walked up the stairs and grabbed the doorknob to enter the building when he froze. Suddenly, he ran back across the street. He remembered what Alicia had said to Natalie before she shot her.

"Bob Pritchard," Julian whispered as he sprinted into the forest. It had just occurred to him that Alicia would kill the guy. Julian ran into the woods.

"Alicia! Alicia! Where are you?" he yelled. But she was nowhere to be found.

48

All That She Is

Alicia sat in the bushes, staring at the greenhouse at the end of the street. It was an old house that looked like one rainstorm away from crashing in on itself. The paint was peeling off the house so badly that it looked like someone had shoved the wooden structure into an oven and forgotten about it. The windows were dirty. An old, rotten wooden bench sat on the front porch, daring anyone brave enough to sit on it.

Suddenly, an older man opened the front door and walked onto the porch. Although he used a cane for support, Alicia recognized his face instantly.

"You old fuck!" she whispered. Her blood was boiling, and her hands started shaking. As a child, she vowed that she would never forget the man who brought hell to her and her father. His pale face haunted her dreams. The man had chased her through so many of her nightmares that she felt that she knew him intimately.

The man tossed a cup full of spit and snuff onto the lawn. Alicia snarled. The man looked frail now like he was struggling mightily with the pains of old age.

"I don't give a fuck if you're three hundred years old. You'll pay just as the others have," Alicia said.

The older man paused on the porch and looked up and down the dark street as if he had heard Alicia's words. Satisfied that no one was out there, he returned to the house.

Alicia pulled the gun from her waist and started in a slow jog towards the house. As she drew closer, she began to hear the voice again.

Yes! It is him! Kill! Kill!

As she approached the house, her mouth began filling with saliva. Alicia was like a hungry animal lusting after its prey. She wanted to see him pleading for his life, begging her for forgiveness. She longed to smell his blood in the air.

With one kick, her foot kicked the door so hard that it tore off its hinges and landed in the poorly lit room. Alicia scanned the room for her target. Finally, her eyes fell on the older man sitting in front of the television. Their eyes met, and the older man reached for something on the side of his recliner. Alicia didn't hesitate and fired three shots into the older man's arm. The man rolled from the chair onto the floor and cried out. Alicia ran to him and stomped on his belly, causing the man to spit a massive clump of chewing tobacco into the air and onto his face.

"I got you motherfucker!"

"Ow! Please. Take whatever you want. Just let me go."

Alicia slapped the man hard on the face.

"You killed my Daddy!"

"What? I don't know what you're talking about."

"Now you're going to pretend you don't recognize me. You redneck bastard!"

"Really! I don't!"

"It doesn't matter."

Alicia put the muzzle of the gun on the man's kneecap and pulled the trigger. The bullet went flying into his flesh, sending a splash of blood into the air.

"AHHHH! Please! What do you want?"

"Think, you old piece of shit! You called the cops on my father for no reason!"

"What?"

"Yeah. You remember."

Alicia placed the muzzle on the other man's knee and pulled the trigger.

"AHHHHHH! PLEASE! PLEASE! I'LL DO ANYTHING! JUST STOP!"

"Do you remember me now?"

"Wait...yes! I remember—the grocery store. I remember. Please, don't shoot anymore."

Alicia started sobbing. That day of pain came rushing back into her mind, crowding her as she towered over the bleeding man beneath her gun.

"You took my father away. And now you have to pay."

A shadow went unnoticed as it moved behind Alicia. Through her tears, she saw the man look past her. She swung the weapon around and pointed it towards the front door. Julian was standing in the doorway.

"Put the weapon down."

Alicia turned around to face the man lying beneath her gun.

"The cops with you?"

"No. Not yet. But judging from the shots I heard as I approached, I imagine it's only a matter of time before one of the neighbors calls them."

"This is the prick that killed my Daddy. For nothing."

"I know."

Julian walked up to Alicia and placed his hand on top of her arm.

"You don't need to do this, Alicia. It's gone far enough."

"I don't care if I die. I miss my Daddy."

"I know. But hasn't there been enough death? Even if you kill the whole world, you'll still have a hole in the center of you."

"Daddy."

"Yes. Your father's gone."

Julian pushed on Alicia's arm until she lowered her weapon.

"Let's get out of here."

Alicia turned to Julian and buried her head in his chest. Softly, she began sobbing.

"I want the pain to stop. I can't take it anymore."

"We'll fix everything. Don't worry."

"I hear voices in my head. Daddy is talking to me, telling me what to do."

"I know."

"But he's gone now. There's just me. Me and the pain."

"And me."

She looked up at Julian.

"That's right, baby. It's me. I'm here with you. No matter what."

Alicia pushed Julian away and aimed the gun at the man on the floor.

"You're lying! You don't love me! You tried to turn me into the police!"

Julian moved closer to her and held out his hand.

"I'm not lying, Alicia. Ever since the day we met, I've always belonged to you. I won't leave. I'm with you until the end."

"You promise?"

"Yes. I promise. Give me the gun."

Reluctantly, Alicia handed the gun to him. She covered her face with her hands and broke down crying.

"Thank God! Crazy bitch! Now, call me an ambulance, boy," the old man said as he tried to lift himself on his elbows.

But Alicia and Julian continued staring into one another's eyes. Julian caressed her face and kissed Alicia gently on the lips.

"I see you," he whispered.

"I see you," she responded.

Julian put his arm around Alicia's shoulder and moved towards the door.

"Hey! You can't leave me like this! I'll die!" yelled the old man. "Hey! Boy! Call me an ambulance!"

Julian paused and kissed Alicia again.

"This is for you, baby."

Julian walked quickly to the man and kneeled over him.

"Open your mouth!"

"No!"

Julian smacked the man with the butt of the gun.

"I said open your fucking mouth!"

Reluctantly, the man opened his mouth, and Julian shoved the gun into the back of his throat.

"For the woman I love," he whispered, pulling the trigger. There was a loud pop. The man's body shook as the bullet entered his mouth and exited his head, splashing his brain on the dirty floor. As smoke drifted from his open mouth, Julian turned to see Alicia staring at him in disbelief. He dropped the weapon beside the man and walked to his girlfriend.

"You do love me."

"I do. Come on, let's go."

Alicia paused.

"Wait. Get the gun."

"Why?"

"We're probably going to need it. The cops are going to come for us."

Julian walked over to the body and retrieved the gun from the floor. After tucking it into his jeans, he took Alicia's hand.

"Let's get out of here."

The two lovers left the old house and disappeared into the darkness of the night.